ARKANSAS HEAT

VOLUME THREE

CINDY'S REVENGE

BY

KAREN MARIE

COLEMAN

ISBN: 978-1-7328314-6-9

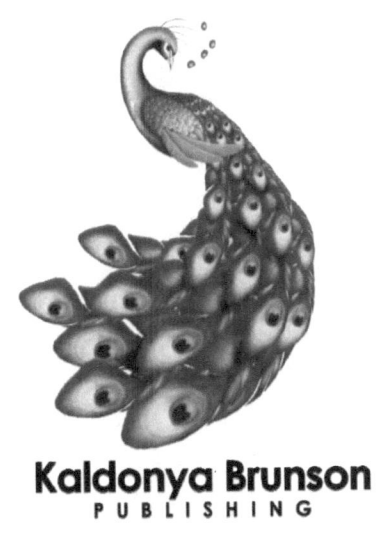

Kaldonya Brunson
PUBLISHING

Email: authorkarencoleman@yahoo.com

Website: www.karencoleman.org

TABLE OF CONTENTS

CHAPTER ONE..5

  ~ JACK'S BACK ~ 17

CHAPTER TWO..44

  ~The Surprise Visit~ 56

CHAPTER THREE 87

CHAPTER FOUR...106

CHAPTER FIVE..119

  ~Amber and Andre~ 131

CHAPTER SIX..158

CHAPTER SEVEN 184

CHAPTER EIGHT 199

CHAPTER NINE...211

  ~THE GRAND REOPENING~ 237

About The Author 239

CHAPTER ONE

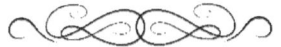

"And they're off!" Thoroughbreds with riders in tow sprinted from their stalls, blasting full speed ahead, each determined to be the first to make it to the finish line. With heavy breathing, their flared nostrils took in as much air as their lungs could hold as they rounded the curve. Their hooves rumbled like thunder, kicking up dirt as they made their way down the track, coming in for the finish. "Come on Lady Belle! Bring it home, girl," Cindy yelled in excitement, rooting for her horse. She crossed her fingers as Lady Belle made her way down the stretch with only a few yards left to go.

It was early spring, and Cindy and Blaine were relaxing in Hot Springs, Arkansas. They were celebrating their second anniversary as a couple and enjoying the city's many spas. They were also having a little fun betting on the horses at the racetrack. Cindy wore a lovely floral sundress with a large white hat and sunglasses. Her long, dark locks flowed in the wind as it blew mildly on a sunny day in March. She was enjoying herself, and she adored her company.

Blaine Cooper, her much-admired lover, is the perfect guy for her. A guy she's always dreamed of having from the moment they met. After many years of friendship, they finally realized they shared a mutual attraction for each other, and since then, they've been seeing each other exclusively. They experienced a couple of trials during their relationship but managed to get through them with love and patience. Blaine is a former police officer and was previously accused of crimes he didn't commit. He had been framed by a sadistic killer and was shot multiple times, severely injuring him. Cindy was instrumental in helping him during the healing process. After a year of rehabilitation and recovering from his injuries, he eventually tracked the real killer, thereby clearing his name. Realizing life was much too short, Cindy and Blaine vowed to put the past behind them and live a joyous and wonderful life together.

Cindy squirmed in her seat as if she were sitting on pins and needles. She leapt to her feet in excitement when Lady Belle made it to the finish line. "Aww Blaine, I won!" She screamed out loud in celebration of her horse's win which netted a huge payout for her. She hugged Blaine and went to collect her winnings. As she walked towards the building, she heard her name being called. She looked around and noticed it was her young cousin Amber. The stunning, young, bi-racial blonde wore a yellow mini-dress that exposed her long, silky legs. She quickly ran over to her, hugging her.

"Hi Cindy," she said, squeezing her tightly. Cindy was surprised but happy to see Amber. The last she heard, Amber was still in law school.

"Amber, hello, oh my god, it's been a minute since I heard from you. You look fantastic. How are you?" Cindy asked.

"I'm great, cousin; how have you been?"

"I'm great. Everything's going fine for me." Cindy, looking her over, said, "Aunt Nancy never mentioned to me that you were home. When did you make it back to Arkansas?"

Amber responded, "I've been here for about a month now. Nobody knows I'm here. Not even Mom and Dad. I'm just lying low resting, you know." Cindy was surprised to hear that Amber had been in town without contacting anyone, especially her parents.

"Are you on a break from law school?" Amber was a bit reluctant to answer the question. She lowered her head as she responded. Her blonde hair was partially covering her face.

She said in a low tone, "No Cindy, I dropped out for a little while. I needed a break from all of that." As they spoke, a man of Cuban descent walked up to Amber, placed his arms around her, and kissed her cheek. Amber was relieved that he'd interrupted their conversation.

"Cindy, I would like you to meet a friend of mine. This is Andre." Cindy's smile immediately turned to a look of disgust and disappointment. The man needed no introduction. Cindy was quite familiar with him. His full name was Andre Delgado.

She was once engaged to his brother Anton Delgado, the head of the notorious Delgado Crime Family. The Delgado family had been career criminals for many years, dating back to his great-grandfather's days, who served in several different criminal organizations.

Their grandfather, Ernesto Delgado, was born in Cuba. He moved his wife to America, settling in Miami, Florida. Ernesto's son Hector was born in America. Hector followed in his father's footsteps, taking over the organization when he died. Their criminal activities included drugs, weapons, extortion, and prostitution. If it was illegal, they were into it, including murder. They would kill anyone at any time. Human life was of little value to them, especially if anyone got in their way. To them, people were so disposable that even certain members of their own family couldn't escape their wrath.

The federal government had begun to close in on Hector Delgado's organization. To avoid a lengthy prison sentence, he chose to testify against his known rivals and several associates. Because of his testimony, millions of dollars in drugs and guns were taken off the streets, and multitudes of murders were solved from America to Cuba. In return, Hector was given a mere slap on the wrist, placed in a witness protection program, and sent to live in a small rural town in Arkansas with his wife and two sons, Anton and Andre Delgado.

The feds relocated the family to the outskirts of a town near England, which consisted of local laidback townsfolk. The population then was less than two thousand, and mostly everyone knew each other. The family stood out from others in the small community as they were the only Cuban family in the town. Naturally, everyone was curious about them since they were new to the area.

Although Hector Delgado was new in town, his criminal activities never ceased. He found it difficult to stray from the lavish, flamboyant lifestyle he'd become accustomed to.

No meager rural existence would hinder him from the pleasures he felt he deserved. He had money hidden in offshore accounts and chose to wait for the perfect opportunity to collect his money. When the timing was right, and he had adapted to his surroundings, he reached out to a few of his old contacts, collected his stash, and continued his criminal organization. Since the town where he resided was too small for him to run his organization, he often traveled the world, leaving his young sons with their mother. When his children got older, he purchased a home among the wealthy in the city of North Little Rock. He blended in quite well and kept a low profile to avoid bringing unwanted attention to himself. They opened a few storefront businesses to *"earn"* legitimate money under their assumed name while trying to throw off the feds. No one in the city knew they were living amongst the likes of a notorious criminal.

One day, while on a business trip to Cuba, Hector Delgado was killed by those seeking vengeance for his betrayal. After the death of their father, the younger Delgado boys would run his criminal enterprise, carrying on his legacy. Their grandfather and their dad were legends in the eyes of the two Delgado boys, and they idolized them.

Many stories were told of their father and their grandfather. Now that their father was dead, they did not need to fear or continue in the witness protection program. They would command respect from the surrounding criminal organizations and rule in their father's stead. They were more ruthless than their father, and there was no loyalty or principles to how they ran their organization. They struck fear in the hearts of even the most notorious of criminals.

As the sons of Hector Delgado, they were idolized by many wanna-be thugs. The police and the FBI had been on their trail for years, but they were so secretive and crafty that they found it difficult to infiltrate the organization. As a result, they continued their criminal activity.

So, when Cindy sees Anton Delgado's brother with her younger cousin, she is greatly concerned. Andre Delgado is a dangerous man. Cindy could only hope that it was simply a date and not at all serious. Amber had been attending a prestigious law school in Connecticut. She was twenty-five years old. Her parents saved most of their lives to ensure that she would be able to attend a great law school, and Cindy was upset to hear that she was no longer attending. She figured Andre was the real reason she was back in town and did not tell anyone.

Andre, knowing Cindy, reached out his hand to shake hers, and in that unmistakable Cuban accent, he said,

"Well, if it isn't my former sister-in-law. You're still incredibly beautiful. How are you?" She refused to shake his hand.

She gave him a grim look and asked, "Andre, what are *you* doing with my cousin?" With a smirk on his face, he said,

"I didn't know she was your cousin; besides, she's an adult. She can make her own choices, right?" Cindy tried to pull her cousin away for a brief chat, but Andre followed. Seeing how happy Amber was, she decided it wasn't the time or place to speak on the subject, so she offered to take her out later. They both agreed and exchanged numbers, and Amber and Andre walked away.

Cindy was concerned for Amber's safety. As she thought more about it, she went inside to collect her winnings and went back outside where Blaine was seated. He noticed the somber expression on her face.

11

"What's wrong darling? Why do you look so sad? You've just won a large amount of money. I would hate to see the look on your face had you lost." She leaned into him slightly, laying her head on his shoulder.

"I'll talk to you about it later," she said. She didn't want to ruin their day, so she did her best to cheer up. After the races, they went to a nice restaurant for dinner and went back to their suite.

They walked into the room and Cindy dropped her purse on the nightstand and pulled her sandals from her feet. Blaine watched as she slowly moped around the room.

"Baby, what's on your mind? Is everything okay?" He walked closer to her and wrapped his arms around her. She allowed him to hold her. His voice calmed her as he spoke in her ear. He had a way of easing her stresses. He has a mild-mannered, motivating personality.

She turned around to face him and said, "I saw my cousin at the racetrack today."

"Oh yeah! Why didn't you introduce us?" She exhaled, then laid her head against his chest and said,

"She was there with my ex's brother Andre Delgado."

"Oh lord, I'm thinking that can't be a good thing."

"You're right. It's not a good thing at all." Blaine knew about the Delgado brothers. He had a few run-ins with them when he was a police officer. They were no strangers to anyone in the state.

"Now I understand why you're upset?"

"Baby, she doesn't know what she's getting herself into. As you know, they're an extremely dangerous family. I was once a part of that family. Anton is an evil man. I'm not sure how I lasted in that relationship as long as I did. Looking back, it was one of the most horrible times in my life. He treated me as if I were his personal property. He was jealous, manipulative, and controlling. Anton once had a business associate who'd made him a lot of money. I mean, this guy was a cool cat. Out of respect, he paid me a genuine and kind compliment. It was nothing tacky or tasteless. I was in the room, and he acknowledged me and everyone else in the room. Anton got so angry with him. He and his men immediately left the house. I looked out of our bedroom window, and they were pushing him into the car. The men, including Anton, got in the vehicle. That guy was never heard from again. From that day forward, none of his men ever gave me a second look. He has a very nasty temper. He loves guns and knives, and he threatened that if I ever left him, he would make me regret it. Going to the police was of no use. One evening, he was pushing me around and fighting with me in the presence of my son. I reached for one of his prized knives, and I stabbed him in the chest.

The puncture wound did extensive damage. He almost died. He covered for me by telling the authorities that a petty thief attacked him. We stayed together, and I helped to nurse him back to health. After he was all better, he got a tattoo with my name on that scar. He used that incident to keep me under his thumb for not turning me over to the authorities. Not long after that, we got into another horrible fight, and he placed a loaded gun to my head and threatened me. I'd had enough. I left, took my son, and hid at my friend's home. She worked for Anton for years, and we'd formed a special bond as she was also my son's nanny. Shortly after moving in with her, I was called home from my job about a fire at our home. That was the house fire in which she and my son died. I had nowhere else to go. Anton came for me, and I went back to him. We continued the relationship for a couple more years. I thought I was in love with him. I had become addicted to the dysfunctional relationship. After the memorial service, I shut everyone out. Anton kept a small stash of cocaine in the home. I began using it to ease the pain of losing my son and my friend. My grandmother was gone, and my family would have nothing to do with me as long as I was with him. I continued to try and numb the pain with the drugs. I came close to overdosing a couple of times. I was of no use to anyone, least of all Anton. He was getting tired of my drug use. He eventually found someone else, and I moved out of his place and on with my life. After a while on the streets, I finally got my life together, went back to school, and got my degrees, and here I am today. I'm not going to say that being with Anton caused me to live that type of lifestyle, but I can tell you it didn't help. Now my cousin is dating his brother. She's dropped out of law school and is hanging out with him. I tell you, nothing good can come of this."

Blaine took her by the hand, and they sat down. "Well, you should speak with her more on the subject because she doesn't need to be in that sort of environment." He stroked her shoulders. "If you need me, you know I'm here for you."

"I know Blaine. Thank you, babe." She showered, pulled herself together, and gave Blaine the attention he and she deserved.

Cindy Brooks grew up on the rough side of town in the housing projects known as the Highland Gates Community. Her life was a true story of perseverance. If anyone ever pulled themselves up by their bootstraps and got on with life, it was Cindy. She owns a successful cabaret-style club and restaurant in the greater Little Rock area. For the past fifteen years, she's been running it alone. It's a popular place with the locals. It's an eatery in the daytime, but in the late evening, it's a cabaret club and restaurant for adults only. Cindy is a poet, and she loves writing sensual erotica and spoken word acted out on stage by some of the most beautiful and talented male and female artists around. She has customers coming from all over the nation. Her guests enjoyed great food and grand performances resembling live shows in Las Vegas, and she spared no expense for production. She rarely took time away from the club, but she decided to trust one of her managers to handle business at her place for a couple of days while she and Blaine took some much-needed time to relax and regroup. Rather than waste time worrying about her cousin, Cindy tried to enjoy the rest of her weekend.

~ JACK'S BACK ~

Jessica Barnes, a former police officer turned private investigator, is a close friend of Cindy and Blaine. She and Blaine were former partners on the police force, and he now works for her as an investigator at her firm. It was a slow day at the Barnes Detective Agency, so Jessica was helping her mother add files to the computer. They were almost done when a large, older black man with greying hair and broad shoulders walked in the door with two bouquets of roses in his arms. He yelled out loud,

"Where's my baby?"

Both Jessica and her mother had their backs turned to the door. Jessica's mother peeped over the counter and saw who had walked in. She pursed her lips and produced a slight frown. The man smiled as he caught a glimpse of her. She quickly turned her back to him and pretended as if she hadn't noticed him. Jessica looked at her mother, who was clearly uninterested in the visitor. She stood to her feet, looked up at him, and exhaled.

"There she is. How's my baby doing?" He walked over to Jessica and gave her a huge, smothering hug.

"Hello, Dad. How many times do I have to tell you that I'm in my forties and no longer a baby?"

"You're never too old to be my baby girl," he said. Jessica pulled back slightly. She was happy to see her father, but she was a bit reluctant to express her excitement, fearing it would upset her mother. Often, she felt they put her in the middle of their tense relationship. She loved them both dearly, but she didn't appreciate the feeling of having to choose one over the other.

"Why, Jessie sweetheart, you don't look like you're happy to see me," her father said while handing her one of the bundles of roses.

"I'm happy to see you; it's just that I wasn't expecting you. Why didn't you call me to let me know you were going to be in town?"

"I wanted to surprise you, sweetheart." Her mother folded her arms and snapped,

"What a surprise this is." He gave her a cheerful smile and said,

"Hello, Annette. These are for you. Girl, you're still as fine as the most expensive bottle of Italian wine." He leaned back, taking in all her beauty. She wore a lavender tank top with spaghetti straps showing her toned arms. pair of yoga pants and gym shoes. How old are you now, about forty-two?"

"Un-um. Don't even try it. Get on away from me with that mess and take your dried-up roses and sorry sentiments with you."

18

She walked into one of the offices in the back while he and Jessica visited.

"Dad, thanks for the roses; they're very lovely. She took her mother's roses and placed them on her desk along with hers.

"What brings you by Daddy?"

"I'm here on business, and I thought that since I haven't seen you in a while, perhaps we could spend some time catching up. Would you like to go out to dinner later?"

"Dinner? Actually, I had plans with my boyfriend Marcus, but I think it would be nice if we could all go out for dinner. Where are you staying?"

"Since I have several meetings in the area next week, I got a suite downtown in the River Market district. I didn't want to impose on anyone."

"If you would've let me know you were coming, I would've set up one of the spare rooms for you. You didn't have to get a hotel. I have plenty of room at my place."

He reached for her hand and gave it a light pat.

"Oh, I'm alright baby. It's better this way. I want to discuss a few important things with you over dinner, and after that, I'll be on my way soon enough."

"How important is it?"

"It's about business, but I'll give you the details at dinner tonight. There are a few things you need to be aware of." He kissed her on the cheek and turned around to walk outdoors. Before doing so, he yelled towards the back at her mother,

"Annette, I'll see you later!" She yelled back,

"Don't count on it." He smiled and said to Jessica,

"She's still quite the fireball, isn't she?"

"Don't worry about Mom. You know how she gets at times." Jessica walked with him.

"I'm looking forward to dinner with you tonight baby."

"I am too, Dad. Where do you want to eat?"

"Ah, you know me; I'm a steak man, so we can go over to the Butcher Shop. That's my favorite spot. In my opinion, they make the best steaks in Little Rock. I know there are plenty of places in town with great steaks, but if it ain't broke, why fix it."

"Yeah, Dad, you've still got that old-school palate. I think it'll be fine. Just call me when you're ready."

Jessica went back into the building. Her mother came from the back with her arms folded.

"What does Jack want?"

"I don't know Mom. He says he wants to talk over dinner tonight. I want to know why you're still so hard on him after all these years?" Her mother took a seat at her desk.

"He knows why."

"But Mom, it's been almost fifteen years; surely he can get a decent hello."

"Well, not until he realizes what he did."

"Mom, you are the wisest woman I know. You've given me more sound advice than I can count. Why don't you follow your own advice and forgive Dad? Whatever he did to you, I know you can find someplace in your heart to forgive him." Her mother looked at her as if she were wasting her time even speaking on the subject.

"I don't want to talk about it, dear. As you said, it was long ago, and I don't even want to think about it. Also, I hate the fact that he feels he can pop up unannounced, barging into our lives whenever he gets ready. He acts as if the sun rises and sets in his asshole. He could've at least given a courtesy phone call; that way, I won't have to be around when he comes. I mean, that's common courtesy. He's just selfish. He's always thinking of his needs, not concerning himself with the needs of others. If you can't meet his desires in a timely manner because you're too busy making a home for his ass, then he goes and screws around with one of your good friends."

There was dead silence. She looked at Jessica as if she'd said too much and walked away. She ran into a back office. Jessica thought, *"So that's why she still hates dad."*

She knew her father had been unfaithful, but she didn't know that he had slept with one of her mother's friends. She went to check on her mother, who was standing next to the window and staring into space. The pain of the past crept up on her and presented itself through her eyes in the form of tears. She'd never actually gotten over the betrayal, as she and Jack were not only best friends, but she felt like they were lovers for life. Since then, she never allowed herself to be in a serious relationship. Jessica went to her mother and took her hand.

"Mom, I'm sorry. I didn't know."

"Of course, you didn't know. Nobody knows. That's nothing you can just tell anyone. I've had to live with the pain all alone. He knew I loved him. Over thirty years of marriage was thrown away because he was too selfish to wait on me. Jack slept with my good friend. Now you know why I hate seeing him. He's never apologized. I think they kept the fling going even after we split. It just ruined us. I had to divorce him. Everything that we'd built together from the ground up was gone in one selfish act. So, when you're feeling sorry for him, remember, I'm not the one who slept around and destroyed our marriage. I know you love your father, and I've never tried to keep you from loving him. I don't mind your relationship with him. I feel that if he wanted a relationship with me, he should've kept his pants zipped. He comes around here smiling and happy with a smug attitude as if nothing had ever happened. I have no reason to smile at him. If he'd been a good husband just as he was a father, we'd still be together."

Jessica allowed her mother to vent for a while. When she was done, Jessica fixed her a cup of coffee. They both went back to work. Jessica thought about what her mother shared with her. She felt a sense of sadness for her. Her mother rarely dated. For years, she threw herself into her work or the aerobics classes she taught at the gym and hung out with her best friend, Mrs. Lancaster. Her mother's a very beautiful woman to be in her sixties. She has a toned body, youthful face, and figure. Her salt and pepper hair was cut in a short pixie style. She and Jessica are often mistaken for sisters.

She has many suitors, but she's never gotten serious with any of them. She's an endless flirt, but that's about it. At the end of the day, she goes home alone. She still lives in the luxury-style home that she and her husband bought together in the Heights. She lives a fulfilling life, and being around Jessica suits her just fine.

After work, Jessica headed home, making a few calls on the way. When she got home, she noticed that her boyfriend Marcus had cleaned the home and had a few things set out to cook for her for dinner. He heard her car come up the driveway, and he met her at the door.

"Good evening, love," he said as he kissed her on the lips. She was happy to see him. They had been dating for almost three years. Initially, she was against having a serious relationship with a man much younger than her, but she decided to give it a try. They managed to stay together, and he moved into her home and rented his condo to wealthy clients who visited the city on business.

"Baby, I took some things out to cook for dinner tonight."

"Oh babe, I'm sorry, I should have called. My dad's in town, and he invited us to dinner tonight. I told him we would be there. I hope you don't mind." He looked at her and smiled. He kissed her lips.

"You know I don't mind. What time is dinner?"

"We need to get ready now. I'll need to shower." He snuggled in closer for a few kisses on her neck.

"Want some company? You know I'm good at washing your back and other things too" he said in between kisses. She smiled and kissed him back.

"I thought you'd never ask. They made love in the shower. He cleansed her body kissing her and playing with her and her him. Their love play was interrupted by her ringing cell phone. She reluctantly got out of the shower to answer it. It was her father.

"Dad, we're on our way," she said, not giving him a chance to talk. She ended the call.

They got dressed and drove to the restaurant. Her father was already there waiting. They greeted him.

"It's good to see you again Mr. Barnes," Marcus said as he shook her father's hand.

"Call me Jack, Marcus." Her father hugged her, and they were seated. After placing their order, her father began to speak.

"Baby, you're looking great, and so do you, Marcus. This young man must be good for you. So, how are things going over there at your company, young man?" Marcus, not wanting to talk business, said,

"Things are going great. How have you been?" he asked, hoping to change the subject. "I've been good. You really ought to let me connect you with some of my business contacts. It could prove to be a lucrative move for a business-smart, bright young man like you. Perhaps make you a millionaire while you're still young. You don't want to wait until you're an old man like me."

"Oh, I'm okay Jack. I'm doing quite well now. But if I need you, I'll let you know okay."

"Okay, but don't wait too long now. If you're going to be with my daughter, I want you two to have a wonderful life together. My baby girl deserves nothing but the best." Jessica said to her father,

"Dad, we're okay. He's doing quite well, and Thanks to you, I am too." Marcus interrupted her, seeing she was a bit uncomfortable talking about finances.

"So Jack, what do you think about those Razorbacks?"

Jack leaned back in his chair and said,

"They're pretty good so far. I'd been keeping an eye on them while I was in Tacoma. They have a pretty great lineup. I can't wait to get to one of the games."

Marcus said, "Yeah, I'm kinda looking forward to going to a couple myself. I have season tickets so if you're interested, you're more than welcome to come along." They talked about sports for a few minutes. Jack shifted the conversation from the Razorbacks to his next subject.

"You know, kids, I'm considering moving back to Arkansas for retirement. Hell, I can catch a game any time. Tacoma is not where I want to be anymore. I decided to come over here to look at some property. I sold my shares in one of my companies and made a nice piece of change in doing so. I've made all the money I could over there. It's time for me to move on and let the young folks have it now. Besides, I thought it would be nice to be close to my daughter."

Hearing that, Jessica wondered how her mother would react to her father's decision to move back to Arkansas.

"Jessica, I have something here for you." He reached into his suit pocket and handed Jessica an envelope. "This is yours. Jessica opened the envelope and saw a check for a generous amount of money.

"Dad, what's this for?"

"It's a little something I'd been saving for my grandchildren, but since you don't seem to want any, I'm giving it to you. You're a smart girl. You can control your own money. Also, you still have your shares in the company. I need you to meet with Alex Thornton about a few things. He has some business contracts for you to look over and sign. He's going to be calling you soon." Alex Thornton is Jack's longtime friend and trusted attorney.

"Okay, Dad."

"In the meantime, I want to get a drink and eat my steak." He hailed their waiter and ordered drinks. Jack Barnes was a jokester, and he was known for telling the funniest stories around. They laughed and talked and enjoyed the night. Afterward, Jack went to his suite, and Jessica and Marcus went home.

The following morning, Jack's attorney called Jessica in for a meeting. She had been waiting for his call. She went by his office. Alex was like an uncle to Jessica. When she was younger, he was always over, and she'd known him all her life because he and her dad were friends long before she was born. Regarding Jack's business, Alex Thornton was a pit bull. He viciously fought for and won many deals on his behalf and helped to close many difficult business deals. He's a brilliant business attorney. It had been about six months since she'd visited his office. She went inside. The receptionist catered to her until Mr. Thornton came out to meet her. With a bald head, he stood at five-nine, wearing a blue plaid suit jacket over a light blue shirt with a bowtie, dress slacks, and designer shoes with a military shine. He was a handsome man with a medium-light skin tone. After greeting her with a warm smile, he gave her a lingering hug. As she pulled away, she was a bit confused by the hug. They proceeded to his office.

The smell of expensive leather-bound law books lined the large office resembling a grand library. The rich, deep wood furniture shone like polished glass, making the office look warm and inviting. They shared a little small talk and proceeded with the meeting. He sat behind his desk with gathered folders filled with legal documents.

"Jessica, Jack is restructuring his will. He has a few financial things here concerning you. As you know, your father is a very wealthy man. Over the years, he's made some significant investments that have proven to be quite lucrative. While our team of financial experts are doing a wonderful job, he wants to involve you in the business aspect of the company. Initially, he'd planned to sell everything, but he's afraid he'd be cutting his family off from the potential of more wealth in the future because these businesses are doing quite well and projected to do even better. He's appointed me as his attorney to oversee these transactions. You and I will make the best decisions for all involved together. This means that your father is turning everything he owns over to you." Jessica looked confused.

"Yeah, but Dad has already given me so much. I'm set for the rest of my life."

"Listen to me, sweetheart. You don't understand. Among all the businesses owned by your fathers, Jack obtained several patents. These patents can potentially make him millions of dollars in the future. He can sell them, but he doesn't want to at this time. He wants to see how they will do in the future, so he's leaving that

29

decision up to you. I'm quite knowledgeable in this field, and I'll guide you as I have him. Allow me to show you what I mean. He handed her all the documents and tried his best to explain to her, going over everything.

"If you choose, you can sell them because they now belong to you. As for now, anyone seeking to use these patents must pay your father's estate royalties. I personally feel that it's in your best interest not to sell anything at this time. I'll walk you through everything, and along with our team, we'll make sure your interests are our number one priority. We will serve you as we've served your father. As I stated, he is restructuring his will, including the latest portfolios and other capital your father now owns.

Since your father's cancer is now in its advanced stage, he's decided to put his personal and financial affairs in order while he's still of a sound mind. That's why you're here."

Jessica was visibly shaken, "Cancer! Dad has Cancer?"

"I'm sorry Jessica, didn't you know?"

"No, I didn't know," she began to sob. Mr. Thornton stood to his feet and hurried to her side to comfort her. There it was—the reason behind that lingering hug—now it was much needed. She held him tight and cried into his chest. After a few minutes, she pulled herself together.

"I'm so sorry sweetheart, but I thought he told you." She sat there stunned. She was speechless. I can see you're upset. I'll give you some time to yourself." He handed her the documents. Look these over and get back to me as soon as you can. I want you to study it well. When you're ready, we'll set up another meeting. We'll go over everything with you with a fine-tooth comb; I'll be here with you, guiding you every step of the way. I see that you and Jack also have some things to discuss."

Jessica took the documents and left. As soon as she was in her car, she called her father. He was at the golf course. "Dad, I need to see you." She drove over to the golf course. They were seated, and he ordered an iced tea for them.

"Dad, I just left Mr. Thornton's office. When were you going to tell me you had cancer?" He looked at her with a disappointed expression on his face.

"I can't believe he told you." She frowned at him and snapped back,

"I can't believe you didn't."

"Baby, I'm an old man. I'm going to die. It was no use in telling you. Why would I? So that you can sit around worrying while counting the days. I know I'm not counting."

"How long, Dad?" He looked at her, knowing what she was asking of him.

"Doc gave me a year, two years tops. This is my second bout with it. When I had it before, I took chemotherapy, and I got better. That was over seven years ago. This time, I don't feel up to all that. I've decided to accept my fate and enjoy my life. I don't want to be in hospitals getting poked and prodded while staying sick from the chemo, radiation, or whatever other toxins they pump you with. I just don't have that in me. I've lived a rich, full life. I want to spend the rest of my days enjoying myself. That means being next to the people I love most. That's you and your mother and my good friends here in Arkansas. I'm going to play golf, eat what I want, drink what I want, and when the good Lord decides it's my time, I'm not going to fight it.

Now, I want you to forgive me for not telling you. I didn't tell you because I love you. I want you to be happy. Enjoy your life as I have. Enjoy the ones you love, and when you find someone special as it seems you have, never betray him or his trust. Hold on to the ones you love and the things you treasure most, and don't allow any outside entity to come between you. I've had much success in my life, but I have one major regret: losing your mother and splitting up my family. If I could change that one thing, I would have been the most successful man in the universe. I should've been a better husband to your mother and a better father to you." She took her father's hand.

32

"Daddy, you were a great father, and you still are. You are a great man. I love you. I know you made a mistake, but you were always there for me. The news of you having cancer saddens me. This is very painful for me. I need time to process this. I wish you had told me."

He squeezed her hand. "That's why I'm here now. I don't want to waste any more time. I want to be around you as much as I can." She smiled through tears that were beginning to fall from her cheeks.

"That's what I want to, Dad." She hugged her father tightly. She didn't want to let go. She didn't want to let him out of her sight. She knew it wasn't possible to spend every waking moment with him. She began to regret all the times she could've spent with him but was too busy with work. She hugged him a little while longer. He allowed her to do so. Jessica had been so busy with her career as a police officer and then a private investigator that she barely made time for anybody. It wasn't until she quit the department and opened her own detective agency that she realized just how obsessed she had been with her career.

While on the police force, she felt that not only was she fighting criminals, but she had also been fighting for change within the department. Change she felt was needed for her and others to do their jobs effectively. Being a black female in law enforcement had its challenges, and she noticed them more and more as she was promoted. She didn't think things would ever change, so she left. She felt her time would be better served working in the private sector. Now that she has her agency, she can use unorthodox methods that usually fall within the grey area of the law's legality. She usually solved most of her cases with that and her keen instincts. She's been working for herself as a private investigator for close to nine years, with her mother right by her side. She only wished she had spent more time with her father. She was determined more than ever not to waste any more time. He patted her lightly on her shoulder as she loosened her embrace. He pushed her long hair from her shoulders and wiped the tears from her face with a napkin.

"Stop your crying. I'm going to be okay, baby. I love you." She looked at him with love and concern. Her brown eyes were red from crying.

"I love you too, Dad." He took his seat again. They talked a little more, and he returned to his golf game. Jessica went to the agency and sat staring out of her window. She watched as people walked by. She thought about her father. She took the documents that Mr. Thornton had given her to review. After spending about an hour reading them, she became overwhelmed by all the paperwork and all the wealth her father had accumulated. Mr. Thornton was right; she would need his assistance to help her with the decision-making process. She dropped her head on her desk and sobbed.

Her mother walked over to comfort her. Jessica didn't talk much about her problems, and she's not known for wearing her emotions on her sleeves, so her mother knew whatever was troubling her had to be big. She went to her desk and touched her shoulder.

"What is it, dear?" her mother asked.

"I'll be okay, Mom." She said without raising her head from her desk.

"If you need me, I'm here." She didn't want to pry, but she knew her daughter had to be hurting something awful for her to break down crying. Her mother tried guessing. The only thing that came to mind was her ex-husband. Out of anger, she asked,

"Did Jack do something?"

"No, Mom." Jessica lifted her head from her desk and looked at her mother. She had swollen eyes and a tear-stained face. She went to the restroom to get herself together.

After coming out, she said, "Mom, I'm going to need to take a few days. Tell Blaine when he and Cindy come back that I won't be in the office for a while, and I'll need him to take over all my cases." Her mother tried to get her to talk about what was bothering her and asked.

"Baby, what's wrong?"

"Mom, I don't want to talk about it." Her mother asked one last question in hopes that she would reveal her troubles.

"Is it Marcus, baby?"

Looking at her mother and feeling agitated, Jessica said, "Mother, no, it's not any of those things."

Jessica got her keys and her purse. She needed to get some air. Leaving everything on her desk, she quickly walked out. She drove over to her favorite park, Willow Beach, to clear her head. As a child, her father would take the family there, and they spent plenty of lazy weekends there on their boat. Sometimes, they'd fish, or other times, they would camp out by the Arkansas River. She parked her vehicle and walked alongside the water's edge. She sat on a nearby bench, looked toward the sky, and began to cry. She questioned God, yelling at the sky as if it could talk back to her. She sat there waiting for answers. In the meantime, her mother was at the agency worrying about her. Not knowing what to do, she sat at Jessica's desk. She noticed the legal documents there. When she saw her ex-husband's name on them, she got angry, and she said aloud, *"I knew it was Jack."* She thumbed through the documents, studying them closely. Being a former paralegal, she understood what the documents meant. Jack had accumulated large amounts of assets. After studying the documents more closely, she noticed he was leaving Jessica his wealth, which she'd always suspected he would. She was puzzled as to why that would upset her daughter. In the event of her father's death, she would become one of the wealthiest women in the state.

She continued probing through the documents until she discovered an envelope addressed to her. She picked it up and stared at it for a moment. She felt she shouldn't open it, but the temptation was far too great. She couldn't resist. She carefully opened it. It revealed that Jack had purchased a tiny resort where they spent their honeymoon. He was leaving it to her. He was leaving her a huge sum of money. She was astonished at the number of assets he was leaving her. After studying the documents further, she noticed a personal letter addressed to her. It read,

My dearest Annette, you are my one true love. It's because of you that I became the man that I did. I hurt you deeply and I have spent the rest of my life regretting it. You didn't deserve the pain I inflicted upon you. My actions were selfish and uncalled for. I never knew how to effectively apologize to you because I was so ashamed of what I had done, and anything I said seemed to make the situation worse. I regret ever hurting you. I pray you can find it in your heart to forgive me, but I really wouldn't blame you if you don't. My prayer for you is that you will find someone who makes you happy. You deserve that; don't spend the rest of your life hating men or refusing to remarry because of my ignorance. I want you to spend the rest of your life in comfort, and I wish I could be there to see you smile. Annette, I love you. I've never stopped loving you. No other woman on this earth could take your place in my heart. The mistakes I made were ones of true regret, and it was torture having lived the rest of my life without you in my arms or without having seen your lovely smile. The very thing that kept me going all those years was knowing I once had the chance to love a truly remarkable lady, and I'm proud of that. I lived every day remembering us. I know these words are of little solace, but they are true and are from my heart. You were there for me from the beginning. All I had accumulated I owed to you. What I didn't leave to our daughter, I left to you. What can I say about our lovely daughter? She's a spitting image of her mother, simply beautiful. She's our greatest gift from God outside of His Son. I wish I had more time on earth, but this cancer is the instrument of my death. I pray for Jessica, and I'm in heaven looking out for her. Well, at least that's where I hope I am. Annette, I love you. Jack."

She closed the envelope and sobbed a little. She was sad to read that he was dying of cancer, and his words moved her toward her. The pain from the past seemed trivial compared to what she was reading. All this time, she blamed him, and rightfully so, but she blamed herself for harboring unforgiveness. Deep inside, she knew she still had feelings for him, but she had been so angry that she refused to allow herself to be in the same room with him. Jack was truly a good man, but he made a terrible mistake, and she felt it was time to talk to him before it was too late. She called his attorney and found out where he was staying. She wasted no time contacting him. Jack was sitting in his room when he got the call from the front desk. He answered the phone.

"Mr. Barnes, a Mrs. Barnes is here to see you." Thinking it was Jessica, he said to the clerk,

"Send her up."

There was a knock at the door. He quickly opened it. When he saw his ex-wife standing there, he was surprised. He smiled.

"Hello, Annette." She stood there for a minute trying to find the words. Seeing him, she wanted to embrace him, but she didn't.

"Would you like to come in?" He stepped back as she made her way inside. He offered her a drink, and she sat down.

"What brings you by?" She didn't want to let on that she knew about the cancer. She was hoping he would mention it.

"I came by because I'm concerned about Jessica. She hasn't been herself today. She ran from the office in tears. Do you know what could be bothering her?" He began to wring his hands.

"Look Annette, I have something I want to tell you. Jessica was supposed to stop by Alex's office to sign some documents. He let a secret out that I had been holding."

"What secret is that?"

"Well, the truth is I have colon cancer. It's come back. I had it before, but with treatment, I was in remission. Now that it's back, I have no desire to go through all that again. I don't think I'm up to it anymore. I just want to live out my days enjoying my life. That's why I decided to move back to Arkansas, so I could live my days with the ones I love most. That's my daughter and my family and close friends. I hadn't planned for anyone to find out. I figured everyone would think it was from old age when I died. I didn't want to alarm anyone, nor did I want anybody to fuss over me."

After hearing him out, she said, "Jack, I'm sorry to hear that. Is there anything I can do for you?" Looking at her and knowing all he had put her through, he said,

"No Annette, I couldn't ask you to do anything for me after all I've done to you." She decided to be straight with him.

"Jack, your unfaithfulness in our marriage was wrong. For years, I hated you because I felt betrayed. You took my family from me. I dreamed of us spending our lives together, but that was taken away. You and I were best friends. We were closer than me and Margaret. That's what hurt the most. I hated you so much back then, but I want you to know that I stopped hating you a while ago when I realized I was still in love with you. I was still angry because you never apologized. I know you have shown remorse, but I thought they were just feelings of regret because you were no longer getting

40

your way. I needed you to feel the pain of loss and isolation I felt when you were lying up with that old hag. I wanted you to pay for what you had done and feel its full weight. But we were spending our years apart, and neither of us truly moved on in our lives. I knew you wanted to reconcile years ago, but I decided against it." He looked at her and exhaled.

"I guess I deserved that."

"Jack, can I be honest with you?"

"Sure, go ahead," he sat straight, curious to know what she was about to tell him.

"The reason I came by today was that I found out about the cancer." He looked at her and said,

"Oh, so Jessie told you."

"No, she didn't tell me. She'd been crying with her head on her desk. I asked her what was bothering her, but she wouldn't say. I was curious, so when she left, I went through the documents. I saw the letter you addressed to me. I read it." He was looking a bit bashful. His deep brown face almost turned red as she told him about it. He poured his feelings into that letter, and knowing she had read it made him feel a bit exposed. He thought he would've been long gone by the time she read it.

41

"You read my letter?" She gave him a warm smile.

"Yes, I read your letter. I was moved."

He said, "You know I meant every word of it."

"Yes, a dying man has no reason to lie."

Jack walked over to where she was sitting. "Thank you, Annie." She looked at him, still smiling, and touched that he's called her by her pet name.

"You haven't called me Annie in years. You know I used to love hearing you call me that."

"I loved saying it. Annie, I'm so sorry for the years of pain I have caused you. Will you forgive me?" She allowed him to take her hand.

"Well, that depends." He looked puzzled.

"What do you mean?"

"Jack, I know I've been hard on you, but I don't want to see anything happen to you. If you're not around, what will Jessie do? And besides, I won't have anyone to fuss at. Can you try to fight this if I'm willing to support you?" He looked a bit surprised at her request.

"You mean you want to help me get better? That's quite the change. There was a time I thought you would welcome the chance to see me in my grave." She looked at him and frowned.

"I don't think that's funny, Jack. I never wanted you dead. I just wanted you to suffer a little. Can we agree to leave the past behind and try to become friends again?" Jack moved in closer.

"Of course, we can. If you can find it in your heart to forgive me, I can at least do what I can to get better." He tried to kiss her on the cheek.

"Not so fast, mister." She smiled and got her purse. He saw her getting ready to leave.

"When will I see you again?" She put her purse over her shoulder and walked towards the door.

"I'll be in touch." He walked her out. He smiled and watched her as she walked away. He was hopeful.

CHAPTER TWO

Jessica was taking a little time off to be with her father. Blaine took over her workload at the agency. Blaine and Jessica had been partners at the police department. He helped to save her life while out on a call. After they both left the department, they remained close friends. He works with her part-time as an investigator. As a computer forensics analyst and an information technology specialist, he used his skills while in the military and law enforcement. He currently runs a consulting firm. He also teaches self-defense and martial arts at the fitness center that he owns. He was in between duties and there wasn't a lot to do at the agency, so he called Cindy to check on her.

"Hey babe, how's it going?" Cindy was happy to hear from him, as always.

"Hi, Sugar, it's a little busy around here; the lunch crowd is starting to come in, so you know how that is."

"Yes, I know. So, what do you want to do tonight?"

"I have several shows tonight, but I can leave after that. What do you have in mind?"

"I was thinking about a late romantic dinner at my place. Are you up to it?" She smiled while holding the phone.

"I wouldn't miss it for the world."

"Okay, I'll see you soon. I love you, Cindy."

"I love you too." Blaine went about his day while Cindy went back to work.

Cindy greeted some of the patrons as it was customary for her to show her face. After making her rounds, she went to her office. Her phone rang. It was her cousin, Amber.

"Hello Amber, how are you?"

"I'm doing great; I want to stop by. I would like to see you. Is it okay if I come over? I'm right around the corner."

Cindy was glad to hear that she wanted to see her. She felt this was an opportunity to speak with her about Andre.

"Sure, come on over. I'm here." After a few minutes, Amber came walking in bright and bubbly. Cindy went to greet her, and they walked to the bar.

"Hi, sweetie. It's so good to see you again. I'm sorry we didn't get a chance to talk more last week."

Amber leaned on the bar and said, "So do I, but I enjoyed hanging with Andre. Girl, that man had me all over the US. It was crazy." Cindy wanted her to stay a while so she could fill her in on her date, so she invited her to eat.

"Would you like to order something from the lunch menu?"

"Oh no, cousin, I'm fine. I'll come back later, though. I don't want to miss tonight's show, and I must have one of your fabulous steaks or perhaps some of your dry-rubbed ribs tonight. I just wanted to stop by to say hello since I was in the neighborhood." Cindy got them an available table, and they were seated.

"I've been away for about three years now. When you've been away for a while, Arkansas seems so small. It's still a beautiful state, though. So, Cindy, tell me, how have things been going around here? I've been seeing your place on TV a lot lately, as well as on social media. You're blowing up."

"Nothing's new; just busier than ever around here. Ever since I began booking hot celebrities to bring their talents with our shows, it's made us quite popular. They see how amazing our shows are, and now it's the place to be or be seen. They're practically beating down our doors wanting to be a part of the shows."

"Yeah, I've been hearing great things." Amber looked around the place, smiling and nodding her head. Impressed, she said, "Wow, look at this place! I can remember when it was just one small building. You've managed to buy the entire city center and turned it into this amazing place. The renovations alone must have cost millions. It's like stepping into a Las Vegas showroom. Very chic and high-end, very glamorous. I'm definitely feeling the vibe." Thank you. It took a lot of hard work and years of dedication. There were some bumpy days in the beginning, but now it's smooth sailing." Cindy was eager to talk with Amber about Andre Delgado, but she first started with small talk.

"Enough about me. Tell me more about you, girly; what have you been up to?"

"As I told you, I took a breather from school. I'm starting to wonder if I even really want to be an attorney."

"Are you kidding? Your parents saved most of their lives to send you to law school. Why would you want to quit? I heard you were doing so well."

"Yeah, but Cindy, that's not where my heart is. That was their vision for me. They decided I was going to be a lawyer, but they never asked me what I wanted. I tried throwing myself into it, and I had fun for a while, but I have other goals I'd like to pursue."

A bit disappointed, Cindy sat back in her seat and asked, "What are you interested in doing?"

"Well, for one, I want to pursue an acting career."

"Acting?" Cindy said, shocked.

"You can't be serious."

"Yes acting, not only can I act, but I can also sing too."

"I know you can sing, but don't you think you could at least get your law degree? And then, if the acting thing doesn't work out for you, you can still have something to fall back on."

"I'll go back one day, but I need a break. I was hoping you would allow me to perform in some productions here with you. Also, I'll be signing up for drama classes at the university. This is the path I want to follow. I have my mind made up, so please don't try to talk me out of it. It's important to me."

Cindy, not wanting her to shut down, left the subject alone. She knew that pressuring anyone when their mind was already made up would only push them farther away, and she didn't want that. Her grandmother did it to her, and the more she pressured her, the more Cindy resisted.

"So, do you think you can give me a shot here?"

"I don't know about that, Amber; I'll have to see. Let me sleep on it."

"OK, but I want you to know I'm just as good as the girls you have here. I'm also a wonderful writer. I love the theater, and soon, I'll be on that big stage." Cindy changed the subject, finally getting to the real subject at hand.

"Amber, you and Andre, how serious is that?"

"Oh, he's just a friend for now but I can tell he wants more than friendship. He's been spoiling me with fancy trips and expensive dinners, and we've only been seeing each other for four weeks. He took me on a private jet to Miami. Do you know he has a condo in Miami, and he owns several nightclubs out there? I mean you should see it. It's amazing. Oh, and check out this bracelet he bought me. I have several more of these at home," Amber said, oozing with excitement.

"Amber, you know I used to date his brother Anton. Andre Delgado is bad news. He's not a good person. He's an extremely dangerous guy, both he and his brother. I think you need to stay away from him."

"Oh Cindy, he's sweet. He's harmless. He's so romantic and so sexy, and he loves spending money on me."

"Amber, where do you think that money comes from?"

"He owns his own businesses."

"Amber sweetie, what you don't know is those businesses are nothing more than fronts for their criminal activities. You really should think about not seeing him again."

49

"But Cindy he's going to help me with my acting career. He's funding my schooling. I don't have to ask my parents for a dime. He says he's going to pay my full tuition. I love you, Cindy, but I'm going to follow my dreams. I have lived my life too long for others; it's time I make my own choices and live with my own decisions."

"Can you live with the fact that the money you'll be receiving comes from criminal activities, like extortion, violence, human trafficking, and possibly even murder?" Amber looked at her incredulously.

"You're just saying that to scare me."

"I'm being honest with you. The Delgado men are dangerous. If you continue seeing Andre, you'll be putting yourself at risk. Besides, they consider their women their personal property. Once they have you, they'll never let you go. I don't think you're ready for that. You're used to dating good guys, but you're in another league now, baby girl, and in the end, you will not like the results." Amber shifted her body around, clearly uninterested. She said,

"Cindy, I'll be okay. I know what I'm doing. I have to go. I'll be back later for dinner." Amber stood to her feet and hugged Cindy.

"Okay, I'll see ya later," Cindy said exhaling.

Cindy knew that Amber would keep seeing Andre and she wasn't happy about it. There was no use in talking to her parents. They were well up in age, and they wouldn't be of any help. Amber's parents were in their late thirties when she was born. She's their only child. Her father is a retired postal service worker, and her mother was a registered nurse working at the University Hospital for over thirty-three years. They were all too excited when Amber went to law school, and she was expected to get her law degree. But now she's dropped out, and to make matters worse, she's dating one of the second most dangerous men in the state of Arkansas, his brother being even more dangerous than he. Cindy felt ill thinking about it.

She wanted to monitor Amber, so she considered allowing her to work at the club. That way, she could keep an eye on her and perhaps convince her to get her life back on the right path.

A few hours passed, and it was time for the dinner crowd and evening shows. Just as she promised, Amber came by for dinner, but she wasn't alone. She was with Andre, who brought his very own guests.

Anton Delgado walked in with a very lovely young woman on his arm. Cindy hadn't seen him in years. She was thrown off kilter seeing her ex. He was five-eleven, very well built, and still very handsome. His dark hair was neatly groomed. He was well-dressed, as usual. It was particularly important to Anton Delgado

51

that he dressed well. He commanded respect when he walked into a room. He loves to portray himself as an established businessman, but he's nothing more than a common criminal.

Although he indeed has some legitimate businesses, all were founded with dirty money. Cindy was alarmed seeing them, but more so, she was slightly offended. She was upset because Amber had brought the Delgado brothers to her place, knowing she would be against it. Not wanting to start any trouble, she did her best to ignore them, including her cousin. She went into her office and called Blaine to tell him what was happening. Blaine went to the club. He called a few of his buddies who worked at the police department to come and sit in the club. Since Delgado was already on their radar, he felt they would be interested in knowing he was there. Cindy tried to calm her nerves. She got the performers in line as usual. They were familiar with their routines. She got dressed for the two shows in which she was the featured act. When she saw Blaine coming in the door, she was relieved. There were a few plain-clothed police officers she recognized. Blaine spotted the Delgado brothers but stayed put.

She went ahead with her show. Her routine was very erotic. She went on stage wearing next to nothing, as usual, reciting the sexiest poetry. The spotlight was shining on her. Her long, dark, satin hair flowed as her full hips swayed to the music, distracting her audience in a seductive dance. Her alluring body tells a sensual story through poetry, moving gracefully with the music. Speaking softly, she seduced her audience with delectable words pouring from her soul.

Delgado was in the audience watching the performance, his eyes fixed on Cindy. He was in a trance and couldn't look away. His date noticed how enthralled he was watching her. She became very jealous. The cute, feisty little redhead moved in closer to kiss him, hoping he would focus on her instead, but he wouldn't allow her to break his concentration.

He watched as his former fiancé performed. She was even more beautiful and glamorous than he'd remembered. He took note of her many fans. He began reminiscing about the days when she was his. He's always been fascinated with her, but when she got hooked on drugs, he found a sense of comfort in the arms of many women. He'd gained respect from being a powerful criminal and instilling fear in everyone he met but still, he could never shake Cindy from his heart. When it came to her, he was weak. Seeing Cindy now and how beautiful she was, he desired to be with her again, and what Delgado wanted, he relentlessly pursued it until he obtained it.

He noticed the nice club she'd built and its success. He wants a piece of the action and Cindy. He continued to watch as her performance ended. When she was done, the audience, including him, gave her a standing ovation.

As the applause ended, he continued standing, hoping she'd noticed him. After Cindy's performance, she went backstage to help the other performers in any way she could. She tried busying herself to buy some time hoping Delgado would leave. After enough time had passed, she went and sat in the audience with Blaine to watch the show but more so to watch the Delgados. Amber came over, beaming with excitement.

"Oh my god, Cindy, that was awesome! You were really good, and you're so beautiful." Cindy nodded her head.

"Thank you," said Cindy. Blaine stood to his feet. He held his hand out to shake Amber's.

"Hello," he said as he shook her hand.

"Hi, I'm Amber. I'm Cindy's cousin."

"It's nice to meet you. Would you like to have a seat?"

"No, I'm here with friends. I just came over to say hello to my cousin." Cindy didn't want to make a scene, so she said nothing more to Amber. She and Blaine watched as she made her way back over to her table. Rather than going out as she and Blaine had initially planned, they decided to stay at the club to watch the Delgados. Delgado watched her the entire time he was there. After sitting in the club for a while, they finally left.

Cindy was relieved there was no incident. She and Blaine went to her home. She couldn't seem to get Delgado off her mind. She didn't know why she felt so anxious about seeing him. She knew he was a bad guy, but she remembered her passion for him. His lovemaking abilities and his charming ways; The passion that Cuban men seemed to possess that lured women in. But they were not all good times. It was her first time seeing him since their break-up many years ago. As she showered, she gathered her thoughts and went to spend time with Blaine. Trying to forget the stressful day she had; she gave herself to her lover completely.

~The Surprise Visit~

Cindy was working in her office when one of her employees came in to tell her she had a visitor. Cindy thought nothing of it. She went to the dining room of the restaurant. When she saw Delgado, she stopped in her tracks. Her heart was beating rapidly. Her mind raced. She wanted to retreat to her office. Seeing him standing there in her club, she had an instant bout of anxiety. Blaine wasn't there, and neither were the other officers. What little security she had at the moment was no match for this evil criminal. She could hear her blood racing through her head, and the pounding of her heart was so intense that she thought it would explode in her chest. She breathed in slowly. Holding her breath for a minute, she exhaled and walked towards him. In a thick Cuban accent, he said with a charming smile,

"Hello Cindy, my love."

He was close enough to her, so he touched her shoulder and kissed her cheek. As she caught a whiff of his signature cologne, she was reminded of that world again—the toxic environment where she was his companion. Instantly, she felt a sense of relief that she was no longer in bondage to him or his jealous ways.

Life with him was traumatic and full of devastating events and life-altering destruction. A life of always looking over her shoulder for police or other criminals seeking the take-over of the Delgado criminal organization. She was finally free and living her life on her terms, and she was happy. She has the man of her dreams, and Delgado's visit is unwelcome. She ducked away as he tried to kiss her other cheek. She gave a simple smile but a facial expression to let him know his presence was unwanted.

"Hello Anton, what are you doing here?"

He looked at her and smiled,

"Hey love, is that any way to treat an old friend?"

"Anton, I'm busy. I don't have time for any distractions. What do you want?"

"I want to say hello. I saw your show last night, and I thought it was great. I'm so glad I stopped by. You know I was thinking about you last night. I couldn't get you off my mind. You know I missed you. Seeing you on that stage last night, you were more beautiful than ever. It was all I could do to keep from going up there. Now I know why I fell in love with you. I see you've gotten your shit together. Perhaps we can go out again."

Cindy looked at him in disgust, feeling like he had lost his mind. She didn't want an audience as her employees and patrons were looking on. She invited him back into her office. She wanted to make it clear she wanted nothing to do with him, and this visit should be his last. Thinking he was making progress and filled with confidence in his ability to persuade others to see things his way, he smiled a wolfish grin when she invited him to her office. She allowed him to continue talking once they made it to her office. He went on and on about how he missed her and what kind of life they could have together. After he was done speaking, she said,

"Anton, I've moved on with my life. What we had in the past should remain in the past. I'm sure you're doing well in your life too. There's no need to try and re-hash something that was lost a long time ago. I have a new life, and I'm doing well. I feel great and want to leave us where we belong; That's in the past." He wasn't impressed with her speech. He shook his head and said,

"I don't want that. I want you. I have a good feeling about us." She had no interest in what he was saying.

"Anton, there will be no us. You left me; I didn't leave you. I didn't bother you or try to hang around and make it something it wasn't. You found someone else, and you moved on, and so did I. I'm glad it worked out the way it did, or I wouldn't be where I am today."

He looked at her, gazing into her eyes. He wanted her to see things his way.

"I didn't want to leave you. You left me no choice. You seemed to be in your own world. You were crying all the time, and there was nothing I could do to make you happy. You were depressed, and you began using drugs so much that you were barely conscious half the time; so, what other choice did you leave me?"

"I was upset about losing my son and my good friend. She was more than just a nanny to my son. Yes, I was devastated when they died unexpectedly. Now I realize I should've gotten professional help and not used drugs to numb the pain. Besides, you were of no use. You were never home. You were always out trying to take over something or whatever it is you do. I don't blame anybody for my drug use but myself. I learned a better way of dealing with my issues, and I got my life together, and I'm doing great now. As far as the possibility of us getting back together, that's never going to happen." He walked up to her and took her by the hand.

He placed it on his chest and said, "Do you remember this?" He showed her a scar on his chest that was covered by a tattoo with her name on it.

"Do you remember how this scar got here? You put this here when you stabbed me right near my heart. I almost died. I put your name on it to remind me of our love. You are always near my heart. You know I saved you from a prison sentence when I lied to the police and told them someone else stabbed me, but it was you who did this to me." He rubbed her hand across it.

"Go ahead, feel it." She quickly withdrew her hand.

"Anton, you were slapping me around, and you were drunk. I couldn't take the chance that you would hurt me or my son, so I did what I had to do to protect myself. I can't take back what happened in the past. Thank you for stopping by, but I think you should go and forget all about me. I have a man who I love very much. I'm finally happy, and I don't need any distractions in my life. So, I suggest you move on." He looked at her as if her suggestion angered him. He began to act as a bully making subtle threats.

"You know baby, I was talking to Andre, and he told me you own this place. You know he's dating that sweet little cousin of yours. She's cute, kinda dizzy though. She's nothing like you. She's not tough or street-smart. You wouldn't want anything bad to happen to her, would you?"

Cindy looked at him gloweringly. She knew the threats were going to continue, as this is how he operates. If he is unable to convince others to see things his way, he makes threats. If that fails, he uses violence. He continued talking.

"Oh, and your little boyfriend, Mr. Blaine Cooper, he's not even a cop anymore. You know, ex-cops have lots of enemies out here on the streets. I hope nothing happens to him."

He changed the subject.

"Cindy darling, I usually know who owns what in this state. I can't believe I'm just now finding out about this place. Perhaps that's because I've been in Miami for the past seven years. It seems you have a nice place here. It's so classy, very elegant. I didn't know you were so business savvy. You could've helped me with my empire. I can see it now, you and me, the king and queen of the South. Royalty, if you will. You have a lot going on here. Looks like you have all of Arkansas eating out of your hands. How much is this place worth? You're sitting on a cash cow in a major metropolis. I'm sure you wouldn't want anything to happen to it. You know tragic fires tend to happen. I find that most businesses never really come back after catastrophic fires, especially those that suffer a complete loss. Your friend died in a tragic fire, didn't she? She was a former employee of mine. She worked for me for years before you got there. What was her name again?" Cindy looked at him in anger.

"Her name is Leslie, you smug bastard," Cindy retorted.

"Are you suggesting that you had something to do with the fire that killed her and my son?"

"Darling no, I would never kill a child, especially not your son. I'm not that cruel."

"You're cruel enough to bring it up. The fire was an accident. It was investigated thoroughly, so why would you bring up something so painful? That's low even for you."

"I was just hoping to inspire you into negotiating. You know I loved you and your son Micah. He was like my son. I remember when you were pregnant with my child. You told me you had a miscarriage, but I really believe you aborted my child when you left. You took a piece of my heart when you did that. I wonder what else you took from me, Cindy. Did you take some of my money because this is a fancy place you have here? Where did you find the money to buy it? You were nothing more than a pauper when I met you. You turned into a useless dope fiend putting more of my coke up your nose than all of America. I thought you were going to put us out of business. Now you're this *great performer* and owner of this club. How much of my money went into buying this place?"

He turned and looked around at the club with a wolfish expression on his face.

"Anton, I didn't take one thin dime from you. When I left you, I was broke. Hell, you made sure of that. After I left, I fell on hard times, but I got myself together. I built this place from the ground up with my blood, sweat, and tears. I got it the honest way. I paid my way through school, I put a business plan together and I presented it to the bank, and they approved my loan. I had some of my own money that I worked for, and I put a down payment along with my bank loan. After my business became successful, I paid back my loan. I don't owe anybody shit and I damn sure don't owe you anything. I took nothing from you, and I want nothing from you."

He looked at her and, almost wanting to insult her, he asked, "How much do you want to sell it for?"

"My place is not for sale, and I want nothing to do with you. Now, I want to make this clear: I want you to leave and never come back here again."

He let out a sinister laugh and said,

"Or what? You're going to get your little ex-cop boyfriend to hurt me?" He laughed even more.

"I saw him out there last night trying to play bodyguard. I also noticed his little cop friends too. You know none of that fazes me. I own this fucking state. You have no idea who you're fucking with, do you? Look at me, I am Anton Delgado.... Delgado bitch! I don't beg. I ask one time, and if I'm turned down, there's no telling what will happen. You'd be surprised at my ability to use the power of persuasion to my advantage. Anyone, and I do mean anyone, will give in to my demands, and that includes you!"

Cindy glared at him. Yelling at him, she asked, "What in the hell do you want, Anton? You're a fucking millionaire. You have everything you could possibly want. Are you so insecure that you feel you have to bully your way into everything? You're a pathetic piece of shit!"

"Darling, that hurts. Why so angry? You should respect me or, at the least, respect the powerful and legendary Delgado name."

"You don't look so powerful to me. You're more like a cheap street thug. If you want my respect, you should stop being a bullying asshole by using threats and fear to get what you want."

With a halfhearted grin, he said,

"Sometimes that's the only thing people understand. You have to use fear to get them to do what you want."

"That's called intimidation," she said. "That's called negotiating," he retorted.

"You know Anton, I don't understand you. I wouldn't want someone who is only with me because they are afraid. I could never enjoy that type of relationship. Are you so obsessed with power that you would settle for that?" He gently grabbed her by the chin; he smiled and said,

"I still love you. We'll be together again; you wait and see. I mean with the death of Blaine and the fire at your club, you're going to need a shoulder to lean on."

"You're one crazy bastard!" she scoffed. He lifted her chin and said, "Yes, you're right, darling. I'm crazy, as you said; I'm crazy for you." He turned and walked out of her office. With much confidence, he said,

"I'll be in touch; tell your little cousin I said hello." Cindy followed him out of her office. She watched as he and his henchmen left the parking lot in two separate vehicles. She got her cell phone and called Blaine.

"Blaine Sugar, are you busy right now?" He could hear the concern in her voice.

"No babe, what's wrong?"

"Anton just left. Can you stop by for a minute, please?"

"I'm on my way." Blaine made his way over to the club. He hurried inside and went to the back where Cindy was. She was seated at her desk. Cindy's club was equipped with security cameras including her office. She showed him the footage of her and Delgado. Blaine called the police. They looked at the video but had nothing to charge him with because the video had no sound. If they were going to go after Delgado, they were going to need to find a charge that would stick. She was told to protect herself and keep her eyes open. Cindy was upset and she was constantly looking over her shoulder.......

Amber had been hanging out with Andre, and she hadn't been in contact with Cindy. Cindy finally was able to contact her, and Amber agreed to come down to talk to her without Andre. Amber rushed into the club and saw Cindy looking upset.

"Cindy, what's wrong?"

Cindy, brooding, asked, "Where have you been? I have been trying to reach you for days."

"I was in Miami with Andre. We just got back in town last night. What's so urgent that you need to see me alone?"

"Look Amber, I'm going to tell you something. I know you're a bit naïve and you can be stubborn at times, but I need you to listen to me."

Cindy got a little rough with her. She gripped her wrist and leaned in closer, getting right in her face.

"You're playing with danger. Anton came by here and he was making threatening statements about you and my club. He is an evil and dangerous man. Cindy told Amber what Anton said to her word for word.

"In other words, Amber, he is basically threatening to kill you if I don't allow him to have my club. Now I need you to stop seeing Andre and stay away from the Delgados. Your life could be in danger." Amber smiled, looking at Cindy, not believing what she was saying.

"Cindy, you've got him all wrong. He's harmless. He's truly a kind man. He donates to many charities. He helps feed the homeless, buying homes and cars for them. We were just at one of his fundraisers the other day. He helps a lot of people. Besides, I don't want to stop seeing Andre. He just got me an apartment in Miami and one in Little Rock. It's so beautiful; you really should see it." She beamed with pride.

"Amber, damn it, listen to me! He's going to kill you if you don't get out now!" She refused to heed her cousin's warning. "You've always been overprotective of me, cousin, but I'm a big girl now. I can take care of myself." She brushed it off, hugged Cindy, and left.

Cindy was frustrated. Her nerves were on edge. She tried to throw herself into her work. She began to get things ready for the evening shows. The performers began showing up. After waiting a while for one of her main performers, Angelica, she was forced to use a stand-in and start the show without her. The night went well. Afterward, Blaine went over to meet with Cindy immediately.

With a somber expression, he sat her down and said,

"Baby, I have some bad news to tell you." Cindy grabbed her chest.

"Is it Amber?"

"No baby, it's not Amber. It's Angelica. The police found her on Chicot Road. She was found with a gunshot wound to her head and her car was set on fire. The police are still investigating." Cindy was horrified.

"Oh no, Blaine!" She burst into tears. Angelica Nelson had been working with Cindy for several years. She was a great performer. She met her when she was on the streets. She talked her into getting her life together, sent her to rehab, and after she was clean, she gave her a job. She was like family to her. Cindy allowed others to close the club without her. She decided not to tell the employees about Angelica. Blaine took her home in his car. She cried all night.

The following day Cindy didn't feel like doing anything. Blaine turned the television on to watch the news. The volume on the TV was low. Cindy heard them talking about the death. "Turn it up a little Blaine." The newscaster was on the scene reporting on the story. *"Police report that the body of a black female was found in a burned-out vehicle here on Chicot Road last night. Police said it appeared she had been shot at least once. Authorities are withholding her name pending notification of her relatives. As the investigation into this case continues, police ask if you know who is responsible for this crime, please contact the Crime Stoppers division at the number on your screen. We'll bring you more as this story continues to develop. Back to you, John."* Blaine turned the volume down on the TV. Cindy was balled into a fetal position. He held her as she continued to cry.

As the days went on, Cindy tried to make sense of things. She went to the memorial service for her friend. The police still hadn't found her killer. Cindy went back to work. She was informed that one of her head chefs had quit. He had been with her since the opening years ago. He called in and said he wouldn't be working there anymore. She never heard from him again. As time went on, about six months, she noticed a lot of her employees were suddenly resigning. About six of them in that time frame quit with no warning. She was forced to hire and train new employees while still trying to maintain her sanity and keep her business flowing. Her customers remained loyal, and they continued coming.

Soon it was discovered that another one of her employees was found dead. This one was in North Little Rock. He was found in his car with a gunshot wound to the head. He was one of her male performers. His name was Michael Heard. She was forced to deal with the death of another employee, and it was a painful one. Michael was a new father, and he was so excited about his brand-new baby boy. She found herself at another funeral within seven months. Cindy couldn't help but feel she was somewhat responsible for the deaths of her employees.

She had a feeling that Anton Delgado was behind the deaths. She had six key employees quit without warning and two dead. It was no coincidence. She knew it was Delgado, but he was in Miami and had been there the entire time. He doesn't have to be in town to get his dirty work done. He was smart enough not to get his hands dirty. He allowed things to die down for about a month, and soon he came to visit. He couldn't resist the urge to let her know in no uncertain terms that he was pulling the strings behind the scenes, but he knew enough not to admit to anything.

He walked into Cindy's place in the middle of the lunch rush hour, bringing his thugs with him. There were about twenty of them. Wanting to cause a nuisance, they managed to order everything on the menu.

Cindy served Delgado's table herself. She slammed his food on the table, and he grabbed her by the arm and asked,

"What took you so long? Are you short of help?" He looked her in the eyes intently, still gripping her arm. He hurled insults at her.

"Look at you, serving tables like the help. I thought you had enough employees around here. Where's your chef? Looks like everyone just up and quit. Are you working with a skeleton crew today?" She looked at him with the brightest smile and said,

"I'm sorry Anton, I don't know what you're talking about. I have plenty of help. Things have never been better around here, and my business has tripled." She snatched her arm away from his grip.

"I simply like to serve assholes personally. I hope you all enjoy your meals. I made it very special with my finest ingredients just for you. Eat up now. Oh, and if you or your men need anything else, just give me a holler okay."

Cindy walked away in confidence. Delgado was embarrassed. He was afraid to eat the meal he ordered but his men ate everything on their plates. Cindy did nothing to the food, but she wanted to play mind games with him. She went to the bar and pretended to be working. She watched Delgado as he stared her down. He couldn't resist a chance at irritating her, so he went to the bar and motioned for her to move in close. She did.

He whispered, "Bitch, I need to talk to you."

She gave him a shitty look and whispered, "About what bitch?" His expression was that of shock. He couldn't believe she dared talk to him in that manner. She wasn't showing any fear, and he was angered by it.

"Who in the fuck do you think you're talking to like that bitch? I'm fucking Anton Delgado! I will never be disrespected, especially not by a fucking cunt like you." She turned slightly sideways and said,

"Anton darling, you used to love this cunt so much." She walked off in the direction of her office. She knew he would follow. He was predictable. His pride wouldn't allow him to sit still, and his ego wouldn't allow him to go without giving his threats. She wanted to get him to talk. Once they made it into her office, he closed the door and took her by the throat.

"Bitch, do you know who you're dealing with?" She was enraged that he put his hands on her. Her jaws clenched. She tried to pry his fingers from around her throat, but he tightened his grip.

"No, tell me." Feeling empowered that she was unable to remove herself from his grasp he said,

"I'm the motherfucker who can make it or break it for you."

"Oh really? I thought you were the short dick motherfucker who loves to eat pussy because you can't please a woman the right way, so you use your money and threats to feel like a real man."

Her comment angered him. Cindy continued to berate him. He slapped her and pushed her onto the desk. He turned her around with her back towards him. He forcefully bent her over and pulled her panties aside. After opening his zipper, he shoved every inch of

72

his massive muscle into her. Her pussy was warm and wet. As he placed himself deeper inside stroking her, he began to reminisce of days when she willingly gave in to him completely. How she would lightly scratch his back and pull him in deeper. As he pumped her, he lost himself in thought. He fucked her with his very soul. Cindy, seeing that he was enjoying himself, didn't fight back, but instead, she taunted him. "I don't feel shit. Let me know when you get in this pussy." His concentration was broken for a brief second by her comments. He wanted her so much. He wanted her to need him as she did when they were together. He held her, and his heart began to melt. He came to himself as Cindy taunted him. This caused him to fuck her aggressively. Cindy wouldn't let up with the insults.

"I know women who have bigger dicks than you, and they can fuck better, too," she said. She continued teasing him until she knew he was about to cum. She moved forward as he was always predictable by the animalistic sounds he would make. She knew he was about to erupt. She moved out of his grip, not allowing him to finish inside her. He reached for his member and began to masturbate. She was disgusted by him. She watched as he rubbed himself to finish the job.

"You're not worthy to cum in this pussy. Look at you. You're like a desperate dog in heat, looking pathetic as shit."

Once he finished, he let out a sigh. She laughed at him. He pulled her hair and asked, "What the fuck are you laughing at?"

"I'm laughing because your attempt to control me with your little stunt has done nothing but make me horny for my man. Now I have to call him so he can finish the job. A job you're clearly not man enough to handle. Thanks for the tease though." He zipped his pants and began to walk out.

"This shit ain't over Cindy. Oh yeah, you have my condolences on your two employees Angelica and Michael. I heard they met with an untimely demise. Now clean this shit up," he said pointing to the semen on the floor. He walked out. She immediately went to her dressing room and cleaned herself.

Cindy knew she hadn't heard the last of him. She didn't discuss the incident with Blaine, nor did she go to the police this time. She knew it was nothing they would do. He would never admit to the killings. There were no witnesses and the employees who quit simply disappeared without a trace. To make matters worse, her cousin was sitting right in the middle of the devil's den, and she refused to leave.

Cindy was angry. She knew she had to do something because he would be back, and there was no telling who would be his next target. She was not about to sit still and wait. She decided she would take action. The only way she could get close to Delgado was to cooperate with him, and that's what she planned on doing. After a week, she called him.

"Hello, my sweetheart. I'm so glad you called. What can I do for you?"

"I'm calling because I'm ready to cooperate with you."

"So, you're ready to come on board huh? I knew you were a smart girl."

"I would at least like to hear what you have to say. I'm not saying I'm sold on the idea, but I'll hear your proposal."

"Okay, sounds good. I'll send someone over to get you now." Cindy ended the call and waited for her ride.

After a twenty-minute drive, they made it to his home in Scott, Arkansas. She was escorted inside. She wasn't all that impressed seeing all the lavish décor and paintings and other upgrades knowing he hadn't put in an ounce of hard work. Running a criminal organization shouldn't be rewarded in this way, she thought. She, on the other hand, has had to work hard for her money so seeing all he'd continued to accumulate by ill-gotten gain pissed her off, and to make matters worse, he wants to capitalize off her hard work. Cindy has given her very life to her club and her other investments. She wasn't about to let anyone take what she had built with her own hands and turn it into something cheap and sleazy. The club was not just Cindy's heart; she loved her employees, too. They were her family. Now two are dead, and many others have left. Life hasn't been the same ever since his arrival. Her life had already been devastated enough by Delgado, and she was going to stop him at all costs. Delgado walked into the room where she was still standing.

"Hello, my love. I see you finally made it. Can I get you something to drink or perhaps a little blow? You know I have plenty if you need it. Uncut, just like you like it."

"No Anton, I don't want anything you have to offer." He smirked.

"Have a seat."

With his smug facial expression and a prideful stance, he'd hoped to remind her of how powerful and wealthy he truly was. Knowing his intentions, she refused to give him the satisfaction.

With a look of disgust, she scanned the room and said, "I see not much has changed since I last saw the place. This shit's a bit outdated. You really ought to hire an interior designer. Someone more informed about the latest décor. Oh, and the place is so dusty. You probably need to speak with your cleaning crew. They're making you look bad. I'm almost afraid to touch anything in here. I don't want to get my clothes dirty." She looked in her seat before sitting down.

"I'm allergic to insects. I hope there aren't any here. You know, cockroaches and such." She stared him in the face. He glared at her while taking a drink from his glass. He began to speak.

"Darling, I don't know why you insist on doing things the hard way. I see after much persuasion, you're ready to go into business with me?" Cindy looked around the room she saw several armed men walking around.

"Well, that all depends. As you know, it's not wise to go into business with someone without seeing the books. For all I know going into business with you could prove to be very costly."

"No, what would be costly is not going into business with me," he snarled. Cindy pulled both her arms up by her side to mock his statement.

"Ooh, the big bad Delgado," she taunted.

"So, tell me, Anton, what do you want from me exactly?"

"I want your club. I don't want to go into business with you. I want to buy it. I want to restructure it. I like the classy scene that you have there, but I want to make it a little sexier. I want to bring more sex to the club. Don't worry, you can still perform your little poetry shit or whatever it is you call that show you do. I just think it needs to be less talk and more sex, more women."

Cindy was angered at the very thought of what he was suggesting.

"Why do you want my club of all the clubs you can have or build?"

"I want your club because you already have the business, and the customers and people trust you. I'm a businessman and I'm always looking for ways to expand my capital. Andre tells me you have a major following. I hear that people fly in from all over just to visit your place. I've heard that some of our friends in Hollywood have visited your place. It's quite popular. Critics have mentioned you in several magazines and a couple of national television shows. That's pretty impressive, especially for a club in Arkansas. I want to get in on the action. I'll allow you to keep your show, as I said, but I want to expand. I want to add on and perhaps make it a strip joint too. That way we can get professional athletes and the music industry to come here. Kinda like my clubs in Miami. I mean you're doing a great job; I just think things could be done better. You're in a great part of town with easy access to the interstates and other things here in the city." Cindy looked at him in disgust.

"You only want my place because you want to control me. You want me to need you so badly. You're like a fucking brat. You put your toys down when you lose interest in them. As long as it's lying there on the floor, you're okay but as soon as someone else comes along and shows interest, you want your toy back. Well, I'm not a fucking toy. I'm not something you can just play with and throw away and pick up when it suits you. I've learned to move on with my life. I started over from nothing. I worked for everything I have. I didn't bully my way into it; I didn't lie, cheat, or steal, nor did I break anyone's legs. I earned every penny."

"Look, I'm willing to buy the club from you. I didn't ask you to give it to me."

She snapped back, "Yes, but when I declined, as it's my right to do so, you had two of my employees murdered, and you scared off most of my workers. Then you come by my place bringing your punk-ass friends and practically raid my restaurant, demanding everything on the menu. Then followed that up with a pathetic rape. Wow, you leave a girl with no options. I hope you're proud of yourself. You call yourself a man, but I beg to differ. Those people you had killed had families and loved ones who cared about them. Michael was a new father, and now his child must grow up without a father. You steal people's lives, and you play games with them like you're some sort of god. There is a special place for guys like you, and trust me, you'll be there sooner than you think."

Cindy stood to her feet. "I'll sell you the club. I'll sign whatever it is I need to sign, and you can have it, but I won't work there. You have to get your own people." Cindy began walking away.

"That's not the deal I'm offering. I won't buy the club if you won't work there."

"Anton, just tell me how in the hell are you going to make me work there?"

He smiled and said,

"As you know, I have my ways. By the way, how is your little cousin Amber doing? She's just so stinkin' cute. She has a beautiful face and such a lovely smile. She's getting on up there in age, but she still has her sweet sexy body. I wonder if her pussy is as good as yours. I may have to find out. Perhaps my men would like to give it a try. You know we love to share around here. She'll have so many dicks in her mouth, that she'll feel like she's had a complete dental overhaul. After they've all had their turn, that little pussy of hers will be like the Grand Canyon. When we're done with our toys, we dispose of them. Now that's what separates the men from the boys; knowing when to dispose of trash."

"Hmm, I see you're resorting to rape. That seems to be the thing you love doing lately. It must be disheartening knowing no woman is willing to sleep with you."

He lit a cigar and called his right-hand man named Wolf. Wolf's a six-foot mass of Cuban muscles and a skilled assassin. He's been with Delgado since the beginning of his criminal career. He does a lot of his dirty work. He'll kill anybody in a heartbeat including women and children. They've been known to shoot in cars and bomb homes, killing entire families or anyone they perceived to be a threat, all on Delgado's orders. Wolf was especially ruthless. He simply didn't care. His father was a small-rate drug dealer who cheated all his customers as well as his friends. He was always in debt and never paid his bills. His mother was a waitress trying to help keep the family together despite his father's shenanigans. One day his father's ways caught up with him. After cheating the wrong people, they went to his home to confront his father. He was around thirteen years old when his parents, his two younger brothers, and an older sister were violently killed in the ambush. He witnessed it all. He was injured but he survived the massacre. He was taken into a youth services facility after being released from the hospital. After turning eighteen, he was released because he was ineligible to live there any longer. He was turned over to the streets with nothing but more than his suitcase. He began hustling on the streets to survive. He turned to all sorts of crimes, even robbery. He killed a couple during a robbery once because they fought back. Losing his entire family turned his heart into evil. He was extremely bitter and had no feelings or empathy for anyone. He felt since it happened to him others should be able to feel the pain he felt. He was callous and cold.

He's been rumored to have an obsession with sleeping with teen girls, and he was hated by many, but when it came to murder, he got the job done without leaving a trace of evidence. He walked into the room. He'd heard everything she and Delgado had been discussing because he was standing guard at the door.

"Yes Delgado," Delgado took a puff of his cigar and said to Wolf,

"See to it that she gets home safe. Make sure nothing happens to her. She and I have a big business deal coming up."

"Okay, Delgado."

Delgado looked at Cindy and said, "Now go home and sleep on it. I'll be in touch." Cindy followed Wolf out. He placed her in the back seat of the SUV. He got in and was seated. She looked at him through the rear-view mirror. Every few minutes he would look up at her.

"So Wolf, how long have you been doing Anton's dirty work? Twenty years now and you're still calling him boss. You're pretty loyal or pretty stupid. I mean, if I were you, I would've branched out a long time ago. I wouldn't sit around spending my life being another motherfucker's flunky. Shit, I wouldn't give a damn how much the job pays. What kinda man stands around like a fucking coward all day waiting to be told what to do by another man? I mean you literally have to hold his dick while he takes a piss. You probably eat the peanuts out of his shit too. What kind of shit is that? Hell, even I managed to get my life together and run a successful establishment. One of which he's trying to take over. I couldn't do it… You're a special kind of stupid. Anton's running all that money through his organization while you and the rest of your co-workers sit around and collect the scraps he throws at y'all like stray mutts. How much does being a fool pay? You have no health benefits or retirement. What're you going to do when you can no longer serve him? Shit, you're supposed to be doing just as well if not better. You're being loyal to a man who knows nothing about loyalty."

He looked at her with an evil smirk. "Cindy, you don't know what you're talking about. You know you're lucky Delgado told me to make sure you got home safe, or I would kill you myself like I killed that little brat of yours." Cindy looked in horror.

"What the fuck did you say?"

"You heard me right bitch. I'm the motherfucker that blew the house up. You had me chasing your ass all over town. Hell, Delgado was looking for you, but I tracked your ass down. I meant to kill you, too, because you were no good for Delgado. So, I waited until it was late when I knew everyone was asleep, and then I made my move. I made it look like an accident. Imagine my surprise when I found out you weren't there. Delgado found you and took you back. Whenever you were around, he would fall off his game costing him millions of dollars. I don't know what the fuck it is about you, but he can't seem to let you go. It's like he's fucking obsessed with you. Now he's back on this bullshit again. He's got me babysitting your ass and killing off your fucking employees and for what? A cheap washed-up two-dollar whore, and a lousy ass club you own just so he can get back with you. He has million-dollar deals going down with major people, and we're back into this petty shit again. I should just kill you anyway, but I'll wait. Oh, and when the time is right, I will kill Delgado and his brother, and I will take over his organization. I'm just waiting for him to sign on to this major deal I have set up for him in Miami. I've been watching him for years. And like any good strategist, you must know when to make your move. Delgado is stupid. I know more than you think I know. Delgado is only as strong as the men who support him. I've managed to gain the loyalty of all his men and as soon as he's dead, they'll come under my rule. Then you'll see that I'm no flunky or an errand boy. Delgado is a slave to pussy and power. What he doesn't know is, that I hold all the power in this organization. I'm the one who actually runs this shit while he flaunts around with every whore he can find. I set up the deals; I kill the right people at the right time. Do you actually think I'm doing all of this for Delgado? Hell no."

Cindy wanted to cry but she was too angry. Her emotions were running wild, and she felt she was coming unglued. She didn't want him to see the horror on her face. She wondered if Delgado knew Wolf killed her son. He already hinted that it was no accident. She was sitting in the back seat listening to Wolf's admission of not only killing her son and her friend but her employees as well, and his intentions were to kill her. She tried her best to remain calm. Wolf flashed a sinister grin while staring directly into her eyes. Pleased with the pain he was inflicting on her, he slowly leaned back in his seat and continued on his route.

She hoped he hadn't noticed how she began to tremble violently trying to hold back her emotions. It was all she could do to keep from attacking him at the moment. She thought of ways to perhaps overpower him, but it was of no use. He was clearly armed, and given his massive size, he'd kill her for sure. Getting him would take careful thought and much planning, so she would wait for the opportune time.

He dropped her off at her club. She got out and slammed the door. She got into her car, sat there for a while, and just cried. She began to think of her son. His name was Micah. He was only four years old when he died. He was her reason for living. She was feeling regret and a sense of guilt that she put her child and her friend in a dangerous predicament. After she cried for a while, she drove herself home. Cindy wouldn't tell Blaine or Jessica of her intentions. She didn't want any interference. She kept quiet. She remained calm. She couldn't afford to lose her head. Especially not now that she has learned the truth. She wanted revenge. She could taste it. It was the very thing that fueled her emotions to carry out her plan of vengeance.

Cindy immediately went into action. She went online and purchased a few GPS tracking devices. She also bought a new laptop, and several burner cell phones. As she was transported to and from weekly meetings with Delgado, she planted a tracking device in the vehicle Wolf drives. It was all she could do to keep from trying to kill him as she rode in the back of the SUV. She held her composure knowing the fate that awaited him. Over the next couple of weeks, she began tracking Wolf's every move. She watched his comings and goings, awaiting the perfect time to exact her revenge. She located his home. She noticed that he lived alone, and not only that, but she also realized he had no security at his place of residence. Using skills she'd picked up when she lived the street life, she was able to break in easily while he was away. She went into his computer to see if she could find anything on Delgado or any evidence of them killing her son or her employees. She found nothing; she did, however, find thousands of pictures of teen girls in compromising photos on his computer. *"Sick bastard! I guess the rumors were true. Fucking old ass pervert."* She turned the computer off, snooped around a little more, and left.

CHAPTER THREE

After getting her father into one of the best cancer treatment facilities, Jessica was back at work full-time. Blaine had been holding down the fort at the agency on the days she was a little busy with her father. He was finally taking the treatments he swore he wouldn't take. Unbeknownst to her, he was taking the treatment because her mom motivated him to do so. She left work a little early and went to her father's apartment to check up on him. She used the spare key he'd given her. She walked inside and heard him with a female. They were flirting and kissing. Both their heads popped up from the sofa. It was her parents. Her mother was topless, and her father was shirtless. Seeing them there together in a compromising position surprised her. She tried covering her eyes, but she had already seen too much so she immediately apologized and backed out of the room. Her parents got dressed and her mother came to the door.

"Hey baby, come on in." Jessica, still in shock, not knowing what to say, came in slowly. She looked for her father. He was standing in the living room looking like a teen with a huge smile on his face. If he died at that moment, he would be a happy man. She noticed the expressions of love and joy on their faces, and she knew they had reconciled. She didn't want to pry but she hoped they were going to continue to be okay with what they were doing. As her mother tried to explain she interrupted her, "Mom, It's none of my business. You don't have to explain."

"I know I don't. We were going to tell you. We just wanted to work through a few things. Your dad and I have become close over the last few months. We've been seeing each other exclusively. We decided to take it slow, but at this point, it's official. Jack has promised me that he'll continue his treatments because we want him to live a long and healthy life."

Her father walked up to her mother and held her from behind as she was still speaking. "Baby we've talked our issues out. I made some mistakes years ago and they cost me dearly. Your mother, with her loving heart, has forgiven me, and she used her love to persuade me to take these treatments. She stood by me every step of the way. I tell you, I don't deserve her, but I thank God for giving me a second chance."

Her parents faced each other and began to kiss as if she weren't in the room. She covered her eyes.

"Y'all, I'm still standing here."

They continued kissing. She turned and walked towards the door. She yelled,

"I love you two, I'm going to work!" She got in her car.

Thinking about her parents, she smiled and shook her head. She was happy to see them both enjoying each other's company. It was good for her to know her mom had forgiven her dad. The two lovers had smiles on their faces and acted like love-crazed teenagers. She began to recall the many times her mother came to the clinic visits, citing she was there to give her support as her dad had his treatments, but she was actually there for her father, too. She said in her audible voice, *"Oh, Mom was real slick pretending she was still pissed at Dad, knowing all along they were secretly seeing each other. Oh, I'm going to get her when I see her again."* She smiled and started her engine and went back to work. A weight was lifted from her shoulders. She pulled into the agency. Blaine was outside in the parking lot talking to Cindy. She pulled next to Cindy's vehicle. It was kind of cool outside. She got out of her vehicle and went over to speak to Cindy.

"Hi Cindy, how have you been?"

"I'm doing wonderful," she lied.

"Why don't you get out and come inside for a minute?"

"Oh, I can't, girl; I'm in a hurry." Cindy didn't want to talk much because she had a lot on her mind.

"How about lunch tomorrow?" Jessica asked.

"I'm sorry but I'm unable to make it. I'm swamped with business, and I don't have the time. I'll call you if anything changes," said Cindy. Cindy really didn't feel like being bothered by anyone, especially Jessica. She was so sharp that she knew she would pry information from Cindy. Information she'd hoped to keep secret.

"Okay," Jessica said.

Jessica went into the building and watched as Blaine continued his conversation with Cindy. He leaned into the vehicle and kissed her. She watched as she drove away. Blaine came inside.

"Whew, it's kind of cool out there today," Blaine said rubbing his hands together.

"Yes, it is mid-October, so the weather tends to get a little cool this time of the year. You know, after the State Fair comes, the weather always gets cold." Tilting his head sideways Blaine looked at her.

"Oh, come on now, Jessie, tell me that you don't believe in that myth too, do you?"

She laughed and said, "What? Everybody knows that the fair brings cold weather. It's been that way since we were kids." Blaine chuckled.

"It does seem that way. I tell you some people swear by it. It's so silly to hear someone actually say it and believe it." Jessica changed the subject.

"Blaine, I haven't been by to see Cindy in a while, how has she been?"

"She she's doing all right, I suppose. She seems to be doing a lot better. She's still coping with the death of Angelica and Michael. She has her good days but there are days she tends to be overwhelmed."

"Yeah, I know that was sad. Blaine, have the police mentioned anything about a possible killer? I mean, do they have any leads? I haven't spoken with Armstrong in a while since all this stuff has happened with my dad."

"I spoke with him a while ago and I can't get anyone to talk. After their deaths, six of Cindy's employees quit, including her main chef. They quit within a week without a word as to why. All of this happened after Delgado came by the club some time back. Seems as if he wants Cindy to go into business with him. He's suggesting that she sell the club to him. He's accusing her of taking some of his money to open the club. He knows it's not true. He's a jealous control freak and he resents the fact that she's happy and living life without him, and now he wants to come back to make her life miserable."

"What? Are you serious Blaine? Why am I just now hearing about this?"

"Jessica, I've been taking on all your cases. I wouldn't dare bother you with any of this."

"Yes, but you guys are my friends. You're practically my family. I always want to be informed of what's going on with you."

"Jessie, as your friend I saw fit to leave you out of it. That way you can focus on your father's well-being."

Jessica smiled and said, "Trust me when I tell you, my dad's going to be okay. Mom's going to see to that."

Looking a bit confused Blaine asked, "What do you mean?"

"When I stopped by earlier to check on him, I caught them making out on the sofa. Apparently, they're seeing each other again. They've been sneaking around for a few months now. It's probably been longer than that. I thought I was going to have to hose them down, I had to leave because they were making out while I was standing there. They couldn't keep their hands off each other," she said with a chuckle.

"My parents are something else. I'm happy for them but I hope they know what they're doing."

Blaine said, "Trust me, at their age, they know what they're doing. That's good news."

"So, tell me more about Delgado and Cindy, What's going on with that?" Blaine sat on the edge of Jessica's desk.

"We know Delgado is behind everything that's happening with Cindy and her club, but as usual, he has an alibi. He was in Miami and to make matters worse, her younger cousin is dating Delgado's young brother Andre. Delgado has made subtle threats, but there is nothing the police can charge him with. I was there the night when he and his crew came by Cindy's club. He didn't start any trouble because he knew better, but he went back the following day like a coward while she was alone, and that's when he began terrorizing her. You know Cindy has a bright fun personality and tenacious spirit. She's sweet but she's firm. Nothing seems to faze her. But since all this has happened, I've seen the pain in her eyes. I hold her every night. She crawls in my arms for the security she needs. I feel as though I'm failing her because although I'm able to protect her from most things, it seems the only monster I can't deliver her from is Delgado. I can't break this invisible connection and I'm not sure she knows how to. It's like he has this crazy hold of fear over her that she won't discuss with me. She seems to think he wants to harm me. She holds me tight every night. She's constantly checking on me to make sure I'm okay and she does the same for her cousin Amber. He uses threats to keep her in line with his sick twisted plan to get her back. I hate seeing her so torn up with emotions. He's slowly killing her spirit. Out of all the things life has thrown at her, she has managed to pick herself up and keep on moving, but lately, she's taken such a severe blow. I plan on doing whatever I can to get something on this guy so that the police can put his ass away for good."

"Blaine, I know you love Cindy. I care about her, too, but going up against Delgado alone is extremely dangerous. Hell, he's managed to elude the authorities for years. You need to let the police handle him. I don't want anything to happen to you. Your body has finally healed from your injuries during the shooting. It hurt me to see you suffer the way you did."

"I'm not going to confront him, Jessie. I've just been asking around a little." Blaine and Jessica continued discussing the subject and went back to work. Blaine went to work in the field and Jessica made some calls.

The following day Jessica and Cindy had lunch. Although Cindy wasn't up to it, she tried to hold a normal conversation, but her mind continued to wander thinking about the Delgados. Jessica questioned her about the events surrounding the deaths of her employees. Not wanting to involve her, Cindy shared minimal information. She was going to deal with Delgado on her own terms and she wanted no interference from Blaine or Jessica. She was painfully aware that the police could do nothing, so she began planning ways to stop him.

After lunch, Cindy contacted an old friend named Big Dan. Due to her former life on the streets, and her involvement with the Delgado criminal organization, she's quite familiar with the criminal underworld. She's maintained some of her connections and has earned respect from those who were involved in the underground life during that era. Big Dan has ties to that world and deals in weaponry of all kinds from automatic assault weapons to many other forms of heavy artillery. He stealthily operates his empire. Only a select few are aware of his ties to the illegal gun trade. To get to Big Dan, you either know him personally or you're a family member.

Cindy and Big Dan share a common bond and have maintained a close friendship to this day. Whenever Cindy was in trouble, he was there for her, and he offered her protection. They used to run together back in her days on the streets. They conducted a lot of business together and she trusted him with her life and he her. The rules of the streets were to trust no man, but they proved their loyalty to each other time and time again. He's a family man. He has six young daughters and no sons. He's married to his wife of fifteen years. He keeps his home-life, and his side hustles separate. His wife doesn't know he's an arms dealer. He attends church regularly with his family, but he still loves his hustle. He's obsessed with motorcycles, and he owns a motorcycle shop where he conducts most of his business. He makes most of his money in firearms.

Cindy met up with Big Dan in Southwest Little Rock at his shop. She pulled into the parking lot. A few guys were hanging outside. Instead of offering motorcycle sales to customers, they were whistling and giving catcalls to Cindy as she made her way up to the front entrance. One of the younger thugs with the nickname "Little Red," namely because he was short and light-skinned with sandy red hair, looked at Cindy as she walked by and said, "Damn, that's one fine-ass bitch." Hoping to gain the admiration of his fellow peers he continued talking about her with disrespect. Cindy looked on in anger. Normally she would give a rebuttal, but she was on a mission, and she had no time for his foolishness. She continued walking. In a flash, she saw his body being slammed to the ground with much force. She noticed Big Dan had picked him up by his jacket. His feet, which bore a pair of Timberlands, were dangling like a rag doll. She looked up at his face. Big Dan still had him by his jacket.

"Apologize to this lady." The face that was once filled with laughter, was now filled with fear and uncertainty. The other guys watched as the scene played out before their eyes. "I said apologize before I blow your fucking head off."

The kid looked at Cindy and said, "I'm sorry ma'am." Cindy nodded her head. Big Dan snatched him aside and slapped him with a hard-backhand blow to the face.

96

"You're the bitch, motherfucker. This is a lady, and a classy one at that." Big Dan looked around at everyone else. He put his hand on the pistol that was in his belt. Because they feared Big Dan, they didn't want any of what he was giving Lil Red. They all apologized to her. Many of the older street hustlers were quite familiar with Cindy, and they knew she was formerly Delgado's girl. She gained some street credibility for that alone, not to mention when she and Big Dan used to run together. The younger generation of street thugs wasn't familiar with her, including this group of guys who were standing outside of Big Dan's business.

Cindy went inside with him. He kissed her on the cheek and hugged her, and they made their way into his office.

"I'm sorry about those fools out there. You know these young fuckers don't have any respect for anybody anymore. Sometimes you gotta show a motherfucker you mean business. They seem to think all women are bitches and whores because of this gangster rap and these fast-ass little girls around here. That's why I keep my daughters on a short leash. I have to keep them away from idiots like that. I keep them in school, church, or other positive activities. They're too busy pursuing goals than boys."

He offered her a seat and took one as well. "So, what brings you by? I haven't seen you in about a year. I came by your place for

97

dinner one evening but I didn't stay long. I had a business meeting with clients, but I didn't see you."

"I've been quite busy lately."

They caught up on old times and had about ten minutes of small talk about the earlier days.

"So, tell me, what's up?" Big Dan asked. Cindy wouldn't tell him as he still had a few people standing around. She looked at them, and he motioned for them to leave. After they were gone, she began to tell him what she needed.

"I'm having a few personal issues, and I need some heat. I must protect myself." Big Dan was aware that Cindy had plenty of wealth and could legally afford her guns. Usually, when someone comes to him for merchandise, it's because they want to fly under the radar. They need guns that can't be traced back to them, as it was with Cindy. Since she was there to see him, he understood what this sale would mean to her.

She followed him to a large garage that housed some old motorcycles and parts. They went into the back room where there was a door that led down the steps and into a small bunker. Since he owned the property, he had this underground room created just for his cache of weapons. He showed her what he had available and if she needed more, he could get it. As a gun enthusiast, she was amazed at the massive stock on display.

"I'm impressed. I see I've come to the right place. You've really stepped up your game. Look at this shit," she said as she handled many of the items on display. She was like a kid in a candy store. She shopped for her favorite weapons like a lady shops for clothes and jewelry. She noticed a small grenade launcher. She chose several grenades, assault rifles with silencers, forty-fives, nine-millimeter handguns, two bulletproof vests, and a small three-eighty automatic. She got a few gun holsters.

"Damn Cindy, looks like you're preparing for war. Who are you going up against?" Cindy tried all the guns for ease of use and comfort. He said to her, "If you ever want to target practice, I have a nice place in Gravel Ridge. I use it for practice often." She looked at him hardly saying a word.

"Oh, I'm good. I don't need any practice. You trained me well. I haven't lost my touch. It's just like riding a bike. You never forget." He threw in some night vision goggles and an array of other combat materials. He placed her weapons in cases for her and had them loaded into the back of her SUV. She reached inside her crossbody bag and pulled out an envelope filled with cash. She placed it in his hand, but he refused the payment. "On the house," he said hugging her.

"Cindy, baby girl, if you need me, don't hesitate to call me, okay."

99

"I just may take you up on that," she said.

"Well, you know I'm here for you. I don't care what it is. I got your back." He helped her in her vehicle and closed her door. He waved at her as she backed out of the parking lot. He gathered his guys and spoke of her.

"That woman is one of the baddest females to ever hit the streets of Little Rock. Y'all lil punk ass thugs running around here talking about y'all are hardcore but she's tougher than all of you motherfuckers put together. She's got heart. She's saved my ass more times than I can count. She knows how to use a gun and a knife, and trust me, she's not afraid of anything or anybody. I've had to shoot my way out of some fucked up situations and that woman was right by my side capping motherfuckers. She knows people too. She ran with the biggest drug cartel in the South. She used to be Delgado's number-one girl. Rumor has it he's still in love with her, so let that shit sink in. She and I have been in many dangerous situations and there were times we were the only ones left standing. So, while y'all are running around disrespecting people, you never know who you're fucking with. Normally she would have handled it herself. Lil Red, you better be glad I stepped in when I did, or you could've had a well-whipped ass or a slit throat. She's just the one to do it. If I see anyone else disrespecting her or any other female, y'all are gonna be eating bullets. And what did I tell y'all about hanging out in this damn parking lot anyway? We might as well tell the police what the fuck we're doing around here. A bunch of thugs

100

hanging around here doesn't look good. I don't like that shit. This is not a hangout spot. Y'all are supposed to be working. Big Dan got his keys and pressed the alarm to his vehicle. He looked at another guy who was one of his head mechanics and yelled,

"Larry, lock this place up around seven." The guy nodded his head and Big Dan drove off.

Cindy made it home with her stash. She called her cousin Randy to help her with her things. Randy acts as security at her home, and his wife is her housekeeper. He also did small jobs for her and oversaw maintenance issues. He ensured her vehicles were cleaned and fueled, her security systems were up to par, and the grounds well-maintained. Whatever was needed for the upkeep of the home, Randy and his wife were in charge, including the shopping, duties Cindy was too busy to do herself. She trusted them. Randy is her cousin on her father's side of the family. She has minimal contact with her parents as they basically disowned her when she was in the street-life. She sees her mother from time to time, but she rarely sees her father as he moves from state to state without giving updates on his contact information. Randy and Cindy attended the same middle and high school. He would look out for her at school even though she really didn't need him to. She was quite fierce and a force to be reckoned with. Normally she was the one to come to the rescue of her friends. She trusted Randy, and throughout her adult years, he stood by her even when she was with Anton Delgado. He was there during the death of her son when she went through her bout with drugs and street hustling, and he never turned his back on her. He himself had committed petty crimes in his youth but was never arrested for any of them so he understood that a person's life could change for the better. She remained on the streets until she got her life together.

He and his wife had always looked after her so when she needed someone to maintain her home, she knew there was no better couple than them. They both quit their dead-end jobs to work for her. She paid them handsome salaries as she was doing quite well for herself with the club and other investments. She introduced them to her financier, who advised them how to wisely invest a little of their salaries so that they wouldn't have to struggle and so they would have some savings for their retirement years.

They were a tight-knit family, and they were good for each other, and it worked for them. Randy was cleaning the garage when Cindy came home. He saw her vehicle coming into the driveway and he waited to see if she needed his assistance. She popped the lever, and the back opened on her SUV. Randy saw the cases lying inside. He didn't know what they contained, nor did he ask. He simply helped her take them inside. Earlier in the day, she had Randy pick up a rental car for her. At her request, the license plates had been removed and she later affixed fictitious plates to the car. He then gave her the set of keys to the rental car.

Cindy went to her bedroom and got a few things out of her closet. She took out a short, sexy, form-fitting red dress and a pair of five-inch heels and placed them on the bed. She quickly showered and got dressed. She combed her hair and then braided it into one long French braid in the back. She pinned what was left into the rest of her hair with a few bobby pins. She placed a long red wig on her head. She's now a redhead. She then put on a black concealed carry holster girdle. She wore no jewelry. She went into her garage and took two handguns out of the case. She placed the handgun inside her holster and put the other in her backpack. She took a few extra clips and placed them in her bag. She waited until nightfall, and she drove towards Scott, Arkansas right past Delgado's place where she had tracked Wolf's car.

She quickly drove by, parked in a dark field, and turned off her headlights. She took out her tablet and waited for it to begin tracking his movement. He would have to pass by her to leave the home. After about twenty minutes the tracker began to move. She saw Wolf's car drive past. She waited for a few seconds, and she started the engine and followed from a distance so as not to draw any attention to herself. She was able to follow him home undetected. She couldn't believe her luck. She watched as he went inside where he stayed the rest of the night. She waited until it was very late. She went up to the door and rang the doorbell. She turned her back to the door.

Wolf got his gun as a precaution. He looked through the peephole and saw a redhead from behind. He could see the outline of her body with the form-fitting dress as it hugged her hips. He got a little excited.

"Yeah, what can I do for you?" he asked through the door. Cindy changed her voice to sound much younger than she was.

"Sir, I'm having car trouble, and I can't reach my parents because my phone died. Can you please help me?" Wolf, thinking this was his opportunity to take advantage of a young girl, wasted no time opening the door. Cindy held her head down; her long red wig was partially covering her face. As soon as the door opened, she began firing shots at him, hitting him in the chest several times. She hit him so fast that he was unable to get a round off. As he stumbled backward into the house, she stepped over the threshold of the door and continued firing center mass. The blast from the bullets caused his large body to fall back, finally hitting the floor. He didn't die right away. She stood over him and said, "Look at me, you sorry ass, bitch-made motherfucker."

He was feeling his life slip away. Although he had taken the lives of many people, at that moment he realized he wasn't ready to die. He looked at her as if he wanted to plead for his life, but due to his injuries, the words escaped him. He was about to meet his maker and Cindy ensured that it would happen in a very swift manner. Her heart was filled with anger, pain, and vengeance. No amount of pleading would have persuaded her to allow him to live. She envisioned the moment she would end his life. Knowing she would get vindication fueled her all the more.

"This is for Ms. Leslie," she said as she fired the gun shooting him once in the chest.

"This is for Micah."

With one last blast to the face, his blood and brain matter splattered all over the furniture and the entry door. His skull was open and bare. She was too angry to be disgusted with all the blood and gore of the kill. She kicked his body and said, "That's for Michael and Angelica. She placed a note on his chest that read, *"This is what happens to child rapists and killers. You can't hurt anyone else's children you sick fuck."* She moved his feet aside and carefully closed the door behind her. She went to the car and left. Nobody heard or saw a thing. Still running on adrenaline, she went home and took off all her clothes.

Feeling nauseated from the kill, she went to the toilet and vomited violently as she began to recall the murder. She showered, fixed a stiff drink, and cried herself to sleep with a picture of her son in her hand.

CHAPTER FOUR

Cindy was awakened by Blaine whispering in her ear. Since she was on edge, her reflexes caused her to hit him with a hard slap to the face. She continued fighting until she realized it was him.

"Whoa baby, it's me," he said, reaching for her hands. She looked at him, focusing on his face. When she realized it was Blaine, she apologized.

"I'm so sorry, baby. You startled me. I wasn't expecting you. What brings you by so early?"

"I know you haven't been feeling well lately, so I thought I'd stop by to see if you'd like to do something special tonight."

As Cindy replayed the previous night's events in her head, she knew her life had changed. She was no longer an innocent member of society whose only crimes were misdemeanors. She's now a killer. When she was younger, she had been in multiple shoot-outs, injuring those who tried to harm her, and she stabbed her ex, but nothing compared to killing someone. She felt very strange for having taken the life of another human being, but when she thought of the many lives Wolf had destroyed, including killing her son, she felt justified. She knew Wolf would never serve a day in prison for his crimes. She couldn't allow him to kill her only child and three good friends and simply walk away unscathed.

She did what she had to do. The police were not going to vindicate them. Wolf would never be able to plea bargain his way out of killing her loved ones. The look on his face played in her mind like a bad movie. The look of desperation in his eyes as she snuffed out his life angered her. She thought, *"How dare he look at me that way after all the pain he'd caused?"* She was the last to see him alive, and she was the instrument of his death. She tried convincing herself that she'd saved more lives by killing Wolf because he would undoubtedly continue killing others.

Feelings of depression overwhelmed her, and she began to cry. Not knowing what was wrong, Blaine could only hold her and try to comfort her.

"Cindy baby, what is it?" She didn't answer.

"I'm here baby. You can talk to me. Is it Delgado?"

"No, I'm just thinking of my son Micah." He noticed she held a photo of him in her left hand. She couldn't eat anything. Her day was filled with darkness, and everything seemed bleak. She felt a sense of satisfaction but was a bit remorseful. She thought of how Wolf gave her the news that he'd murdered her child. He was so cold and evil. He bragged about killing a four-year-old child without a hint of remorse. She cried a little more. She didn't want to be alone, so Blaine stayed by her side. She didn't go to the club. Blaine was sitting on the sofa channel surfing. Cindy sat next to him. He stopped on the news channel. They were talking about the death of Wolf. The mailman told his story to news reporters. He told the authorities that he noticed blood on the entry door as he was delivering the mail and notified the police. The police found the note that Cindy left with the body. Although the authorities knew him as Delgado's right-hand man, they assumed his killer was an angry father who had come calling.

Blaine looked at Cindy and asked, "Do you know him?" Cindy, with an expression of guilt on her face, faced him but couldn't bring herself to look him in the eyes.

"Yes, he's Delgado's favorite hitman. It's a shame what happened to him. I guess karma really is a bitch." She motioned for him to change the channel. She didn't feel like discussing the subject. She felt herself getting emotional. She quickly changed the subject.

"Blaine, I'm thinking about temporarily closing the club for a few weeks. What do you think?"

"Why would you do that?"

"Because I don't want anyone else to get hurt. I don't think Anton is going to let up. If I closed the place, he wouldn't have anyone to harass. Perhaps he'll leave us alone."

Concerned for her, Blaine said, "I don't think that'll stop him. You need to go to the police and let them help you."

108

"Nah, the police can't do anything, and even if they did, it would only be a slap on the wrist. He wouldn't serve a day in jail even if they had proof. He would probably be offered a deal. I think the best thing for me to do for the time being is to close. I think he'll lose interest. I feel my employees are being targeted, and I think there will be more attempts on their lives. I want to protect them from any further harm. Also, I'm concerned for Amber's safety. She's so enthralled with Andre that she won't even consider ending their relationship. All she sees are dollar signs and opportunities. Do you know that he's purchased her a place in Miami and here in Little Rock? He's showering her with all this money but not telling her where it's coming from. I know they seem to be legit now, but that money has a trail that can be traced back to illegal activities. I can only imagine how many people he had to shake down to get what he has or, even worse, had murdered."

"Babe, if you feel that closing the club is what you should do, then I support you."

Cindy looked at him and said, "Yes. I don't want anything else to happen on my account." Cindy's mind was made up.

Over the next few days, she got her business affairs in order. She paid off the bills and temporarily closed. She called a meeting with the employees to let them know they would still be paid, but it was a matter of urgency that she closed. She gave them no explanation other than to say she was doing a few renovations.

She waited to hear from Delgado to see what he would try to do. She thought, why wait for him when she can find him and end his threats for good? But that would prove difficult given the army of men he always kept around him. She continued her planning. In the meantime, she called Amber, who was in Miami. Cindy would use her knowledge to gain useful information concerning the Delgados. Amber answered the phone, happy as usual.

"Hi cousin, how are you doing?"

"I'm doing fine, Amber. How about you?"

"I'm doing great; I love this Miami weather. It's so cold in Arkansas, but it's nice here. I love my apartment. I have a lovely place on the eighteenth floor overlooking the ocean. You ought to see it. I'm mostly here alone, though. Andre hardly ever comes to see me. He usually sends a car for me, but it's been about a week since I heard from him. He said a close friend of theirs died in Arkansas, so I haven't gotten a chance to spend any time with him. But who cares? If he's footing the bill, he doesn't have to call. I'm getting a little lonely out here, though."

"Well, how about I come out there on vacation? I need some time away from Arkansas, and I had to close the club down due to structural damage. It can't be reopened until the issue has been fixed, so it's closed for now."

"Oh, sounds like a bummer. Are you okay?"

"Oh yes, everything will be fine. So, do you feel like entertaining your big cousin for a few days?"

"That sounds like a wonderful idea. When can you come?"

"I have my bags packed. I'll be driving, so I could be there in a few days."

"Oh, why drive, cousin? Just book a flight?"

"I just need to take the drive and clear my head. I'm not in a hurry. I want to enjoy the ride, and besides, I don't feel like being cooped up with a bunch of people on an airplane."

Cindy intended to bring her weapons, find Delgado, and make him pay for his crimes against her. The two women continued making plans. Amber wanted to show Cindy she was a big girl, that she would be okay, and that she shouldn't be worried about her. She also wanted to show her a good time during her stay. Cindy, however, packed for the trip, but she wasn't planning on having fun. It was all business for her.

Delgado and his crew held a memorial service for Wolf. It was a private ceremony. His death was not considered to be related to his criminal activities in the Delgado organization. Actually, Delgado sought to cover up what he thought was the real reason Wolf was killed. He didn't want word getting out that this well-known tough guy was possibly killed by an angry parent or an average Joe for fear of his guys appearing weak in the eyes of many. After the memorial service, they all went back to Delgado's place.

Delgado had a big meeting that Wolf had set up with another criminal named Cassias "Cash" White. This agreement would take Delgado's criminal empire to another level. With Cash's Columbian connections as well as Delgado's contacts, both men would become the largest criminal organization in the region and would be the top two drug lords. He couldn't afford anything to go wrong with this deal. The fact that Wolf had set it up kind of worried Delgado, thinking that Cash would cancel the meeting. Since the deal proved to be lucrative, Cash decided to go ahead and work with Delgado. The meeting was set for that weekend. Everything was on schedule.

Cindy said goodbye to Blaine and left for Miami. She checked into a hotel, put her things in her room, and asked not to be disturbed, opting out of any cleaning or room services. She didn't want anyone snooping through her things or finding her weapons. She took out a nice sundress and freshened up. Afterwards, she called Amber. She got directions to her place and drove over. Amber was excited to see Cindy.

"Hi Cuz, it's so good to see you." They hugged.

"Come in, Cindy. She showed Cindy around.

"Amber, this is a nice place. I can see why you love it here."

"Well, come on, let me show you to your room."

"No sweetie, I have my own place, which is not too far from here."

"Why did you do that?"

"Amber, this is your place funded with ill-gotten gain, and I won't be staying anywhere the Delgados are paying. No, I think it's best that I have my own suite. But I wanted to see you. So, how are things going with you here in Miami? Have you found any acting opportunities?"

"Not really; I've been studying, though. I had a couple of auditions for a few commercials, but I haven't found anything solid. Until a few weeks ago, I had been traveling with Andre. Now they're paying respects to their friend, and they're getting ready for this big business deal with somebody they call Cash. It's supposed to be life-changing."

Cindy asked, "Is his name Cassius White?"

"Yes, that's his name: Cassius White."

Cindy knew this was who Wolf was talking about the night he'd taken her home. She thought to herself, "Cash is bad for business. He's even more evil than the Delgados and all other crime syndicates combined. If Delgado is thinking of going into business with him, he would be taking a major risk."

She said, "You'd think that Anton would know better than to go into business with someone like Cash as evil as he is, but I guess he's looking at the money side of things. It must be a good deal for him to continue with the meeting despite Wolf's death." She looked at Amber and asked,

"Amber, did they say when this meeting was to take place?"

"Andre told me it would be Saturday."

"That figures."

"Cindy, you talk as if you know something about this."

"Amber, I know these people. I was engaged to Anton, but I'm not here to talk about them. I'm here to enjoy a little time with my cousin, so let's go and get lunch and perhaps do a little shopping."

Cindy spent the afternoon with Amber. Afterwards, she called Blaine and went to her suite. She got her duffle bag and took a taxi to the car rental place. She stopped in a secluded location and changed clothes in the car. She wore all black. She took out her red wig and went driving. She went to Delgado's mansion. She was familiar with the place. Seeing the house brought back memories, but they were not all good. She and her son Micah spent a lot of time there. She ached in her soul as she remembered her son running around the mansion.

It was nightfall, so she took the night vision binoculars out and watched the place until just before daylight. She changed her clothes and went back to her hotel. She didn't use the valet service; she parked the car herself. She took her bag and went inside. She thought about Micah and went to sleep.

When she woke, she got a couple of sandwiches she purchased the day before and ate alone in her room. She had a video chat with Blaine and met with Amber. At midnight, she went to watch Delgado's home again; she did this every night until Saturday. It was late in the evening. She saw a trail of SUVs pulling up in Delgado's driveway. Delgado and his men stepped within her line of sight. She wasn't visible to any of them. She took out her assault rifle and placed the silencer on it. She moved over to the vehicle's passenger side and peered through the scope. Cash stepped out of the vehicle, and Delgado was there to meet him. She honed in on Delgado and took the shot. She missed him, but she continued firing in his direction. She hit Cash, who was shaking hands with Delgado. Cash was killed instantly. She continued firing, aiming at Delgado, but his men covered him and moved him out of the way. Surprised by the attack, they assessed the injured instead of looking for the shooter. She quickly moved into the driver's seat as they took cover. She slowly drove away. It was a surprise attack. In total, she shot eight men, killing three of them, Cash and one of his men, and one of Delgado's men. They never saw who the shooter was.

She went to an automatic car wash and drove into a stall. While the vehicle was being washed, she changed her clothes, and then she drove back to her hotel and parked it. She was angry that she didn't kill Delgado. She was nervous. She knew she made a mistake and couldn't go back to try it again. Later she turned to the news to see what was being said. The killing had already made the news. Not only did it make the local news, but it also made the national news. She was relieved to find that no one saw her. Even still, she wanted Delgado. It was eating her up inside. She tried to rest but was eager to plan her next move. She imagined many ways of killing him. She wouldn't rest until she got him.

When word got out that there was a shooting at the Delgado compound and that Cash was dead. Many people began to speculate that Delgado was the one who set Cash up to be killed especially those in Cash's camp. They assumed Delgado had Cash assassinated so he could take over his syndicate making him number one in the region. He would control everything with Cash out of the way.

There began to be strife between Cash's people and Delgado's, and a bitter war began. Delgado was on the hit list of everyone seeking revenge for the death of Cash.

They began to attack his businesses and every home he was known to own in the Miami area. They bombed all his nightclubs and the big house in Miami where Cash was killed. Delgado struck back even harder. The more he fought, the worse things got for him. He lost about forty of his best guys and other employees in a two-week time frame. There was so much killing that people were afraid that innocent bystanders would get hurt.

The FBI knew about the two organizations and stepped up its surveillance. Soon, Delgado was forced to leave Miami and go back to Arkansas to lay low for a while. He knew Cash's guys would never give up looking for him.

Cindy was enjoying the fact that Delgado was on the run and hiding out. She could always tell their location because Andre follows Delgado, and Amber follows Andre. He and Delgado were in Arkansas, which was okay with her. Nobody else knew where they were, not even the police. Amber was in her place in Little Rock, which Andre provided. Cindy was glad to know that she was back, but she still wanted her away from him. Amber knew the situation was dire when she saw how anxious Delgado and Andre were about getting back to Arkansas. She, too, was afraid. She expressed her concerns to her cousin, and she was seriously thinking about leaving Andre. She realized, through all that had been happening, that he was more than just a businessman when the violence began to unfold. She didn't like all the guns and the secrecy she was witnessing. She only saw the glamour and the business side of the Delgado operation. She noticed all the gunplay and the violence after the Cash incident.

Cindy was home still plotting ways to get Delgado, and she was going to use Amber to do it. Amber knew exactly where both men were staying, and with her knowledge, Cindy was determined to get him soon.

CHAPTER FIVE

Jessica and her mother were visiting with her mom's best friend, Mrs. Lancaster, for a Sunday dinner. They'd been friends since before Jessica was born. Mrs. Lancaster had twin sons, Chad and Nigel, who grew up with Jessica. Chad had been engaged to a lovely young lady named Blaire Kensington. She was the daughter of a prominent businessman and oil tycoon. She was tragically killed by his brother Nigel, who was serving a life sentence at Tucker Maximum Security Prison in Arkansas. Chad lived between Little Rock and Miami, as he owned a business and condo there. He designs and sells yachts and owns one of the largest marinas and restaurants in the city. Since the main hub of his business is in Little Rock, Arkansas, he'd often traveled between the two cities. He planned on being in Arkansas for a few weeks and Jessica was looking forward to seeing him. Chad's brother Nigel has a daughter with a young lady named Danielle and she was coming in town from Brinkley to the dinner too. Everyone began arriving. Chad walked in. Jessica was delighted to see him. She stood back while he said hello to his mother. He walked over to her and hugged Jessica.

"Hey there, girl," he said, squeezing her tight.

"Hi Chad, I haven't seen you in about six months. It's so good to see you. You always smell so good," she said. He held both her hands and stepped back, looking at her.

"You look amazing, Jessie."

"So do you. So, how are things going in Miami?"

"Things are going well. I'm getting more business than ever. I've had to hire a few more designers, and I've been asked to do a reality show for my business. Can you imagine that? I've gotten multiple offers to appear in dating shows and other reality options."

I turned them down though. Since Blaire's death, I think the public is still following my story. I thought all the interest would die down after a while, but they're still interested in the story. I live a simple enough life, so I don't see how they could find me that interesting.

Jessica smiled and said, "I guess they recognize what those of us who love you have known all along. You're talented, very handsome, and one amazing guy. You were engaged to one of the wealthiest socialites of our day, and you and her father are still close to this day. Plus, the story of your brother. The public is interested. We've been following the stories here in Arkansas."

"I think they're seeing dollar signs. Trust me, I'm not that interesting." They wanted a little privacy to chat, so they walked towards the patio.

"So, how are you really doing?" she asked. Chad lowered his head while thinking about his former fiancée.

"It's been almost three years since the death of my beloved Blaire. I'm coping. I take it one day at a time. I used to wreck my brain thinking about what could've been, but it was driving me nuts. I had to accept the fact that she's gone, and I had to cope the best way I knew how."

Looking concerned for him, she asks, "So you're doing a little better now?" Not wanting her to worry about him, he smiled a little.

"Yes, I think I am."

"Have you been to see Nigel since he's been in prison?" Chad looked a bit disappointed. He really didn't want to answer the question.

"No, Jessica. He's my brother, and I know I'm supposed to love him, but the way he betrayed me by killing my fiancé and my unborn child, I haven't found it in my heart to go and see him. I don't know what type of feelings I would have. I think that seeing him would only rip the scab off my wound, and I would need to go through the healing process all over again. I'm afraid that I may do something to hurt him. My anger has subsided some, but I don't think I'm ready to face him. I still love him, though, and I miss us.

121

He's my twin brother, and we did share a lot of great times, and I enjoyed our friendship. He's always going to be my brother, and I can't change that, but I'd rather not go and see him just yet."

Jessica placed her hand over his, "That's perfectly understandable."

They were interrupted by everyone coming into the room. Danielle had arrived with her and Nigel's daughter Miracle. Since he's serving a life sentence, Chad takes care of his brother's child. He gives her a monthly stipend from Nigel's former business which Chad took over when he went to prison. Danielle walked into the room and hugged Chad then Jessica. It was Danielle's testimony and cooperation with Jessica and the police department that helped to commit Nigel to prison. Everyone was grateful she came forth with the truth. Miracle was standing there in a black and white polka dot dress. She had long, soft, curly hair with a big black and white ribbon in it. Her big, beautiful eyes had lashes that seemed to go on forever. She headed straight to her uncle Chad as he always had gifts for her. She ran to him and jumped in his lap.

"Wow little lady, you sure are getting big. Show your uncle how old you are now."

Miracle held up four fingers. "I'm four years old, Uncle Chad."

"Wow! Four years old, you're a big girl now."

"Yes, I can tie my own shoes, and I help my mommy clean my room, don't I, Mommy?" she said, looking for her mother to verify her story.

"Yes, you do Miracle."

"Well look at what Uncle Chad got you." He got a large bag filled with toys and showed them to her. She leapt with joy, tearing through the bag and playing with her uncle and grandmother. Jessica and Danielle chatted in the background. Jessica talks with her by phone about every three months.

"So, how have you been doing lately girl?"

"I've been doing fine. I've been as busy as ever at the childcare centers. You know I opened another one in Forrest City, and I'll have the grand opening of my third one in West Memphis. How have you been doing?"

"You know me, still doing my thing at the agency."

"That's good. Hey Jessica, I want to ask you something. I need you to give me your honest opinion."

"Okay, what is it?"

"Some of the children have been talking about their fathers at the daycare. Miracle is beginning to ask questions about her dad. I don't want to tell her that he's in prison. I've never spoken with her about him, but she will want to know. I cannot take my baby down to the prison to see him. I've sent him pictures. I know I promised him that if he turned himself in, I would allow him to see her, but I feel that taking her to a maximum-security prison is not the right thing to do at this time. Now, I plan on telling her about him when she's much older, but what do I tell her in the meantime?"

"I'm not a mother, so I don't feel qualified to give you any advice on this. Perhaps tell her daddy is gone for a while, and by the time she gets old enough to understand, tell her he did something bad and must pay for it. By the time she's old enough to understand, you may want to try having her write him letters, then perhaps phone calls. I'm sure when she is older, she will seek him out and want to visit him. In the meantime, continue being the wonderful mother you've been."

"I've been dancing around the subject, and I don't want to hurt her with the truth, but I can't very well lie to her either. Perhaps I'll seek healthy counseling to see my options on the subject. I don't want her growing up feeling like she missed out on something in life. She's so loving, trusting, and innocent and I would hate to ruin all that with a dose of reality."

"I understand what you mean. Have you begun dating again?" Danielle looked at Jessica with a slight frown on her face.

"Jessica, after being with Nigel, I've chosen not to date for a while. I must consider Miracle now, and I can't allow some selfish asshole around me and my baby." Jessica tried to reassure her.

"Danielle, you know not all men are like Nigel. There are some good guys out there who will love you the right way."

Danielle shook her head, "Girl, after being with Nigel and suffering the things he put me through and me almost going to prison, I'll stay single. I'm going to focus on raising my baby and running my business. Besides, she has her uncle Chad and her grandparents. Chad has been great and spends lots of quality time with her. He's been so good to us. He's truly a good man. I wish I had met him instead of his brother. I mean, how two people who are identical can be so different is beyond me. They are like night and day."

While they were still talking, Mrs. Lancaster announced it was time to eat. They all walked into the dining room and enjoyed a wonderful meal together. After dinner, they sat around and talked. Jessica excused herself. She hugged everyone goodbye and went home. Her boyfriend Marcus was out of town on business and wasn't expected to be home for a couple of days. She got a tub of strawberry ice cream out of the fridge and settled in to watch a night of movies on Netflix, and went to sleep.

The following morning, she went to visit her father. He was doing great, getting ready for his chemo treatment. Her mother was right there by his side. She looked at both of them. Her mother fussed over him, helping him get dressed. He smiled at her because he enjoyed the attention. While she was busy trying to help him, he kissed and hugged her.

"Boy, stop it, we're going to be late. There'll be plenty of time for that later."

"Aww, come on, baby, just one kiss," he begged. She stopped what she was doing and gave him a few kisses on the lips. He held her as if it were his last time. "I could love you forever," he said. "I thank the Lord for you, Annette." She smiled and kissed him some more. Jessica looked on, smiling at them.

"You guys are too much."

"Hey baby," her father said. She hugged him.

"Hi, Dad, good morning, Mother."

"Hi, Jessie. Girl, I'm trying to help this old man get dressed, but he's been chasing me all morning; I can hardly get anything done. How are you doing this morning?"

"I'm doing well. I knew Dad had chemo today, so I wanted to check on him. I see he's in good hands."

"Yes, I'm in good hands, baby. This young lady looks out for me. She makes sure I'm eating right and everything. She's even got me doing that juicing thing. I got myself a prescription for that medical marijuana. I have a healthy appetite, but she won't let me eat my favorite foods though. But that's okay. She even has me exercising. Can you believe that? Your daddy, at his age, is in the gym. But I feel much stronger and so much better since she's been showing me how to eat and exercise. My blood cell count is good, and it looks like I'm winning the battle against cancer." Her mother kissed him.

"You will beat this thing. And when you do," she leaned in and whispered something in his ear. He looked at her in amazement.

He asked, "Are you serious? Don't play with me, Annie."

She smiled and said, "I'm serious, now let's do this."

Jessica didn't know what her mother had promised her father, but she was sure that whatever it was, it would give him the strength to move mountains. He strutted around the room with a huge smile on his face. He began gathering his things to leave. He hugged Jessica, and they left, leaving her standing there. She tidied her father's place and left for the office.

Her mom was with her dad at the clinic, and Blaine was at his place of business. She only had a couple of other people with her

127

at the agency. She didn't want to bother them, so she answered the phones herself. Something her mother usually does. Since she didn't know exactly how long her mother would be out, she thought about hiring a receptionist part-time so she could focus more on her cases.

The Barnes Detective Agency helped to solve a major, highly publicized crime, which netted her more clients. People had been coming to her from all walks of life. She was inundated with requests. She had to hire several more people, including a few investigators. She would give the smaller cases to them, but she took on the major ones herself.

As she was sitting at her desk, she began thinking about her boyfriend Marcus. She wanted to call him, but she was unsure if he was in a business meeting, so she texted him that she missed him. He quickly responded with a few flirtatious texts and told her he was looking forward to a romantic evening with her. She smiled and went to work. Once she was done working, she let everyone go home, and she went home herself to set up for a romantic evening with her man. She stopped by the lingerie shop in the mall to pick up a few items. She went to her favorite store and purchased new aromatherapy candles and massage oils. She made it home and got dinner ready. She set the mood in the bedroom by lighting candles and playing soft music. Marcus walked in just in time for dinner. Jessica was lounging on the couch in her lingerie. The lights were low.

He looked her way, "Well, hello there, handsome. I've been anxiously awaiting your arrival." When he saw her, his knees went weak. He smiled and dropped his briefcase at the door. He made his way to the sofa.

"Hello, beautiful. You sure are looking lovely this evening. You look as if you're ready to play." He kissed her. He longed for this moment, and he thought of her often as he was in his meetings. Things got heated pretty quickly. She regained her composure but barely. She wanted him. Not just a little, but all of him. Once they began, they would need no interruptions. She was going to make this young sexual god put in much work, as her body needed all the attention he could give. "Baby, I have your dinner waiting. Go and freshen up." He kissed her and quickly showered. She was in the dining room. He walked behind her and pressed his hips against her ass. She felt his member poking her, which made her want him.

He kissed her ear and whispered, "We can put this shit in the microwave for later. I want you now." She smiled, and he turned her around and passionately kissed her. He lifted her, carrying her into their bedroom. He gently laid her on the bed and kissed her body. He licked her nipples that stood erect. She smiled and moaned as he made his way to her wetness. He kissed her warmness and got excited tasting her sweet nectar. He fed on her pussy as if it sustained the power of life. He loved her with everything in him. She thrust her hips forward as his tongue quickly moved over her erect clitoris. He lifted her buttocks from the bed, and with both cheeks in his hands, she was in mid-air, and he sucked her until her body exploded and he devoured her juices, licking her clean. Her body went limp. Her body was open. She needed him. She opened her eyes and saw his erection. She began to salivate as she saw how hard and perfect it was. It was a huge dark brown with the perfect shaft. She wanted it in her mouth. She was torn between sucking him or fucking him, and she allowed him to briskly fuck her. She wanted to reward him for causing her extreme pleasure. As he began to pound away at her pussy, she stopped him and sucked him.

She could feel the head swelling in her mouth. She slipped her fingers into her pussy while he fondled her breast. Without warning, he released his load. She pushed forward and allowed his dick to go deeper into her throat. She swallowed, and her throat muscles milked his dick of all its substance. He screamed her name. She loved it. She created a sucking sensation as he exited her mouth. His head popped out. She looked at him as if she was ready for more. She lay on her back and squeezed her breasts together. He straddled her face and placed his dick in her mouth until he was fully erect. Thinking of what she had done, he pulled out of her mouth, flipped her body over, and fucked her briskly until he pounded her so hard that she almost begged him to stop. But it was only because she wanted the feeling to last. As he continued, she arched her back, and he hit every erotic spot she had. They loved each other into the night.

~Amber and Andre~

Cindy's club had been closed for a few weeks. She continued to pay her employees as promised. She had no problem meeting payroll because it wasn't her only source of income. She had other business capital from various resources. She conducted her business from home until she could take care of Delgado. She felt it was unlikely that he would harass her at the time because he had far bigger problems than her not selling him her club.

He was trying to stay alive. Even still, she kept the club closed as a safety precaution for her patrons and employees. She was making phone calls and doing more research. She called Amber. Amber was with Andre at their hiding spot. Andre was in another room in a private meeting with his brother. It was incredibly quiet in the place because everyone was on high alert. The ringing of her phone broke the silence. She quickly answered.

She noticed Andre had come into the room at that very minute and stood near the doorway, staring at her, which made her nervous. "Hello," Cindy's voice said on the other end.

"Hello, Amber."

"Hi there, cousin."

"Are you home? I want to stop by?"

"No, I'm not home now. I probably won't be there until tomorrow. Why, what's up?"

"I want to see you." Andre was still standing in the room, watching her closely. He shrugged his shoulders as to ask why she was still on the phone.

"Cousin, I'm gonna have to call you back."

"Wait a minute, when will you be coming home?"

Andre was angry because she wouldn't get off the phone. He went over to her, violently snatched her phone away from her ear, and ended the call. He angrily threw it at her, hitting her in the chest with it. She dared to say a word to him about it. She turned the phone off. Andre began yelling at her.

"Can't you see we're in here trying to take care of business?" He glared at her angrily and then walked away. Andre had never been aggressive towards her. She was beginning to regret that she went with him, but he showed up at her place unannounced. He all but demanded that she get dressed and come along with him. She was planning to discuss that she was no longer interested in seeing him but knowing that he was a part of this crime family, she wondered if it would be a fatal mistake to do so. She sat back in her seat and stayed there until Andre was finished. He came into the room and got her. He saw she was upset about the way he'd treated her. He tried to smooth things over with her.

"Look baby, I'm sorry about what happened earlier, but you must understand everyone's on edge. We were having an important meeting, and your cell phone was disturbing us. You know how my brother gets when he's handling business. He already felt that you shouldn't have been here, but I wanted my girl with me. From this day on, when you're with me, just turn your phone off, and please stay out of the way."

"I had no idea that my phone would cause such anger in you," she said.

"Things are kind of rough for my brother and me right now. You know that. He's lost a lot of his employees due to a misunderstanding. We had a meeting with an important guy. That man was killed during that meeting. His people want revenge, so they're fighting us. I don't want to get you involved in our personal affairs, so that's all I'm going to tell you. People are dying, and that's why we're here in Arkansas. We're trying to keep everyone safe around us. Please understand that."

Amber was sure she wanted nothing to do with Andre, but she didn't know how to go about telling him. He leaned in and kissed her. It wasn't the same. She had fallen for Andre more so for the money, but that's because, at the time, she didn't know who he truly was. She heard her cousin's voice playing in her head, warning her to leave him alone. Now, she was wishing she had heeded her warning. She wanted out but Andre was in love with her. He took her by the hand and led her to the garage, and they left, heading back to her apartment. She was relieved to be back at her place. She placed her things on her coffee table. He was directly behind her. Noticing she was still in a bad mood; he took her by the arm and tried apologizing to her again. He tried kissing her passionately as he had done many times before. She rejected his kiss and walked away from him. Her response angered him.

He grabbed her by the arm and said, "Bitch, where do you think you're going? Don't you ever walk away from me again, do you hear me? You don't want to piss me off. Now, you need to grow the fuck up and quit acting like a fucking brat."

She was visibly shaken as the monster she saw at the house; she was seeing again.

"You will respect me as long as you're with me. Now get your ass over here and act like a woman. Hell; I got a lot on my mind while trying to stay alive and figure out who is out to get us. I'm constantly looking over my fucking shoulder because there's a hit out on me and my brother. I'm trying to love you and keep you protected, and you're running around like a child. This is the real world. You know what type of business I'm in. You know what I do is very important, so yeah, my life and yours are at stake. I've given you just about everything you asked for, making sure you're comfortable—the finest of clothes and cars and an extensive bank account. I could've chosen any woman to share all this with, but I chose you. I may love you, but that doesn't mean I will allow you to disrespect me."

He kissed her on the lips. She was too afraid to reject him, so she kissed him back, but it lacked the passion he was used to. He undressed her and walked her to the bedroom. He lifted her body and laid her on the bed. She knew they were about to have sex, and she wanted to get it over quickly. She tried to reach inside her nightstand drawer for her condoms. He stopped her. With the looming death threats on his life, he was no longer feeling invincible. He had never been married, and he had no children. He said, "I love you, Amber. I want you to have my child. I don't want to use protection. I want you to give me a son to carry my name."

Although initially, Amber liked Andre, she had in no way considered having children with him. Amber felt their love affair was not serious. She was unaware that Andre was in it for the long haul. Since he was always on the go, he rarely spent time with her due to the demands of his criminal lifestyle. She had no other place to go. Andre had paid for everything, and she was so busy spending his money, that she never thought of having to live without it. It was fast money, and she had gotten so caught up in the luxury of having it. She had been having fun, but she'd been playing in the den of the devil, and she was unaware that it came with a hefty price.

He proceeded to have sex with her; she was upset that he wasn't using a condom. After he was finished, she immediately ran to the bathroom to wash up. He walked in behind her.

"What are you doing?"

"I'm about to clean myself."

"Just take a shower. Don't rinse my seed out of you." She looked at him. She was angry that he was making this demand.

He got in the shower with her to make sure she wouldn't. She saw he was getting a bit obsessed, and she was disturbed by his erratic behavior. By now, the romance was completely gone, and she felt hopeless. She showered and tried to get dressed, but he insisted that they make love the entire day. She was exhausted. He finally went to sleep. She went into the living room and sobbed. She felt trapped and thought of what Cindy had said. The Delgado men are dangerous. They think of their women as their possessions, and she was experiencing it firsthand. She fell asleep on the sofa.

The next morning, Andre awakened her as he was going to the restroom. She went into the kitchen and pretended to fix breakfast. He came in and hugged her and kissed her. She cringed at his touch. She poured him a glass of orange juice and handed it to him. Her bubbly personality had been replaced with a solemn, depressed mood.

"What's wrong, baby?" he asked. She pretended to be happy. She hid her feelings.

"Oh, nothing. I just have a lot on my mind."

"You'll be okay. Just go shopping or something. That always seems to cheer you up." He drank his juice and got dressed. He made a few phone calls and left in a hurry. Before he walked out, he looked at her and said,

"Don't do anything stupid." He kissed her and left.

She quickly closed the door behind him. She immediately went into the restroom, got her feminine hygiene product from under the cabinet, and thoroughly cleaned herself. She searched the internet, looking to find where she could purchase the morning-after pill. She wanted no part of being pregnant. She found a pharmacy that carried it, and she stopped by and purchased it. She purchased some bottled water and took it before exiting the store. Her cell phone rang. It was Cindy. She was yelling on the phone.

"Amber, I've been worried about you. What's going on?" Amber was relieved to hear Cindy's voice.

"Cousin, where are you? I need to talk to someone."

"I'm home. Where do you want to meet?"

"Can I come over?"

"Sure, come on over." Cindy anxiously waited for Amber. She knew she was in some trouble. Amber was at the door. She ran inside and hugged Cindy crying. Cindy was relieved to see she was physically okay. Cindy walked her into the living area, where they were seated. She got her some tissues.

"Cindy, you warned me about Andre, but I refused to listen. I wanted so badly to believe he was a great guy, but he's nothing more than a rich thug. Yesterday, while we were talking on the phone, he took my phone, turned it off, and threw it at me, hitting me with it. Then he tried to apologize, but the damage had already been done. He got upset with me because I wouldn't accept his apology. He was cursing me and calling me a bitch. I've never had a guy act that way with me before. He says he's on edge because somebody is trying to kill him and Anton. He says some important guy got killed, and they want revenge. That's why we had to come back to Arkansas. If that's not bad enough, he wanted to make love to me without using a condom. He said he wants me to have his baby. He even followed me to the bathroom and watched me shower so I couldn't thoroughly clean myself. He was acting strange all evening. We had sex multiple times, and it was horrible. It wasn't the same." Cindy moved in close to comfort her as she began sobbing.

"So, what are you going to do, honey?"

"I don't know what to do. I don't want to see him anymore."

"Well, you know he's not going to let that happen. Those men think of women as property. You have taken too many gifts from him. He's purchased you two condos, cars, jewelry clothes, and expensive trips. He thinks that's what makes his woman happy, and you accepted those things. In his mind, you're his. He would never do that for someone he wasn't serious about. He buys his dates a few trinkets and sends them on their way, but he's chosen to spoil you, and he keeps you close to him. I know him. I know when he's really into a woman. When I noticed the types of things he was doing for you, I knew he wanted a deeper relationship with you. On the other hand, you thought you were just having casual dates with a wealthy guy, but he's a dangerous criminal. I know you couldn't see it in the beginning. They're such smooth-talking, suave, and sexy men. I fell for Anton. They're so sweet and charming, and they know how to say the right things at the right moments. Their words are very poetic and intoxicating. It's hard saying no to them. Most women would kill to be where you are. He knows that, which further makes him feel entitled to anything he wants. You were all over him, making him feel like a god. He enjoys your beauty and your youthfulness.

Andre is well into his late thirties, possibly forties, and having a young lady in her twenties in love with him thrills him. And yes, he wants babies with you. If you give him children, you and your children will forever be his property. You would never be rid of him. Life as you know it would be over. I'm so glad I never had

139

children with Anton. Although we don't have any children, he still manages to come around here years later and cause total chaos in my world. Whenever the Delgados are around, people's lives are in danger.

Let me tell you something. I hope you are ready to hear this. If not, I'm going to tell you anyway. Anton came to my club. He says he wants to buy it. I refused to sell it to him. Soon after my refusal, two of my employees were found dead. Both were murdered. A host of others disappeared without warning. Anton came by and all but admitted he did it. He had this smug look on his face when discussing their deaths. Afterward, he made a comment about you. He was warning me that you would be next. They're dangerous killers, honey, and you're going to have to stay away from him. The thing is, even if Andre loves you, if Anton wants you dead, he'll kill you anyway. He won't spare you just because his brother loves you. He'll kill you in his presence and they'll carry your body out and bury you never to be heard from again. Your life is in danger. Even if you run and hide, it's only a matter of time before they find you. You're in too deep just to walk away."

"So, what am I supposed to do cousin? I'm scared."

"I think you need to lay low for a while. Stay away from him for a few days. Anton doesn't know where I live. You can stay here with me for a while if you want. But it won't be long before he tracks you down. I've been waiting for Anton to pop up on my doorstep, but he hasn't so far. If all else fails, you can live at Blaine's place. I think you need to stay away from your apartment for now."

"Cindy, am I supposed to go on the run forever? You said it's been years and you're still dealing with his brother. How can you deal with that? I can't be on the run for the rest of my life. I want to become an actress. How can I do that if I'm in hiding? I can't do this. I'm just going to go to the police."

Cindy asked, "And what are you going to tell them? Don't you know that going to the police will do nothing but speed up your death? Do you know they've never been brought up on charges? Anybody who's ever gone to the police dies, and all witnesses disappear forever without a trace. You don't know who you're dealing with, sweetheart. They will kill you and the police will never find your body. If they do find your remains, it will be because the Delgados want to send a message to others. They are skilled at killing and getting away with it. No honey, going to the police is useless. You've let him know where your parents live, He'll start by trying to harm them, and then if he can't get your attention that way, he will kill you.

Cindy knew she needed to kill Andre before he realized Amber was gone. Her aunt and uncle could be in danger. Amber seemed to be aware of the ramifications of being in a relationship

141

with Andre. She regretted having ever met him. She was in over her head. Cindy didn't tell Amber her plans. She borrowed her cell phone and placed a tracking device inside without her knowing. She wasn't sure her cousin was sincere about leaving Andre alone. Besides the Delgados had a way of convincing women to go along with their plans even if they didn't want to. She could follow her and find out where they were hiding.

Amber went to pick up a few things from her apartment. In the process of doing so, Andre came by. He saw her packing. She hadn't noticed that he walked in, so she was startled when she heard him say, "Darling, are you planning a trip?" She quickly made up a story.

"Yes, I was hoping you would take me to Miami. I have an audition for a stage production there." He looked at her as if he were in a hurry.

"Well, it looks like you're going to miss your audition because we won't be going to Miami any time soon."

"Why is that, Andre?"

"Because something has come up, and we aren't able to go to Miami at this time. It'll be some time before we can go back out there. We're having some problems with a few people there."

"Andre, I don't know many people in Miami so are you saying I can't go either?"

"That's what I'm saying. You're my girl. If I'm having problems, then so are you." Amber sat on the bed. He looked at her stuff and said, "Well at least you're not packing in vain. Get your things. You're coming with me."

"Where are we going, Andre?"

"We have another place nobody knows about. We're going there for a while."

"How long will we be there?"

"Indefinitely, now quit asking all these damn questions, and let's go."

Knowing it would be dangerous to fight with him, Amber reluctantly left with him. She was upset. She wanted to call Cindy, but she knew she couldn't do it in his presence, so she waited until they got to where they were going. The last time she used her phone in his presence, he took it from her. Her phone was her link to the outside world. They drove out of Little Rock and drove towards Conway. After a brief while, they were near Russellville. They got off an exit and drove for about twenty minutes. Amber was becoming alarmed because she couldn't see any homes for miles, only backwoods. Finally, after a few more minutes, they drove up to a private dirt road with walls of trees on either side of the driveway that led to an extremely large luxurious cabin. There were two smaller cabins on the property. She hadn't been there before. The area was secluded. There were no neighbors for miles. The armed men who guarded the place resembled secret service agents with neatly pressed suits and Bluetooth earpieces, with several guns each: the whole nine yards. When they saw it was Andre, they waved him on through. Several people were already there including Delgado. She and Andre went to one of the smaller cabins. He showed her around the place.

"This is where we'll be staying. You can't have any visitors here. Please do not tell anybody where we are. If you want to live, you will not say anything. I'll need your cell phone too. So, hand it over."

"Oh, I didn't bring my cell phone. I left it at my apartment. I was looking for it in the vehicle on the way over. But I realized I left it on my bed as I was packing. Will I be able to contact my family to let them know I'm okay? They'll be looking to hear from me."

"You can call them another time. In the meantime, I'm going to the main cabin to handle some business with my brother. I'll be back in about an hour. You may as well make yourself comfortable. We're going to be here for a while."

Amber was upset. She began to sulk. She walked around the cabin looking at things. The place was beautiful, but she didn't care about that. All she could think of was getting away. She was staring out of the window watching the armed guards. She wanted to get out of there. She kept hearing Cindy's voice playing over and over in her head. "Damn, if I would've listened sooner, I wouldn't be in this predicament." She hadn't left her phone at her apartment. She had it on her, but she didn't tell Andre because she didn't want him to take it. As soon as he was out of sight, she went to the bathroom and called Cindy. Cindy answered immediately. "Cindy, I'm so glad you answered. I went to the apartment to get some things, and Andre came while I was there. He brought me to this cabin somewhere near Russellville. I'm not sure where we are now. He said we're gonna be here for a while. What am I going to do? I can't call the police and tell them where I am. He asked for my phone, but I told him I didn't have it. I told him I left it back at my place."

"Amber, calm down and listen to me. Whatever you do, don't turn your phone off. It can be tracked. Put it on silent and do everything he tells you to do. I'm coming for you. Give me a couple of days. Do you think you can hold on for that long?"

"I don't know cousin."

"Amber, he doesn't want to harm you. You're his lady. As long as you play your part, you'll live. If he wants to make love to you, do it. You say you wanted to be an actress, so this is the role of your life. If you want to live, you must convince him that you love him, and you want to be there with him, and he'll be putty in your hands."

145

"I don't know cousin, but I'll try."

"You can do this, Amber, not only for your safety but for the safety of your parents as well."

"I gotta go, Cindy. Someone's coming!" Amber abruptly ended the call. She came out of the bathroom and saw a beautiful, well-built Cuban American woman cleaning just outside the bathroom door. The lady seemed startled by Amber's appearance in the cabin.

"Who are you, ma'am?" She asked Amber.

"I'm here with Andre. Where did you come from?"

"I was out back doing some work."

"How long will you be working because I want some peace and quiet?" asked Amber.

"I'll be done in about an hour, but I must get dinner started."

"Do you ever leave, or do you live here?"

"No, I stay on the property in the cabin in the back when I'm requested. I take care of Mr. Delgado when he's here."

"How often is that, because I've never been here before, and we've been together for almost a year?"

"Ma'am, I'm sorry, but I don't discuss Mr. Delgado's personal business. What do you want for dinner?"

"I'm not hungry."

"Suit yourself. My name is Rita. If you need me, you can call me on the intercom. I'll be right here."

The worker finished her house cleaning and then went into the kitchen to start dinner. Amber placed her phone on silent and hid it in her bag. She heard Andre coming in. She gathered her feelings and put them aside, pretending to be her normal self. When he came inside, she was all over him as she was when they first began dating. She was flirting and talking, but she noticed he wasn't his normal self. He seemed aloof. He was startled at the slightest sound. Although she told Rita she wasn't hungry, when dinner came, she drank a glass of wine, ate a dinner roll and a salad, and watched Andre play with his food.

"Andre baby, you've hardly touched your dinner. Is everything okay?"

"I have a lot on my mind right now."

"Would you like to tell me about it?"

"Even if I did want to discuss it with you, there's nothing you can do, so to answer your question, no, I don't want to talk about it."

"Okay, well, I'm here." The phone rang inside the cabin. Rita answered it.

147

"Sir, it's Mr. Delgado. He says it's urgent." Andre answered the phone. He listened for a few minutes, and then he yelled out,

"Damn it, Anton! Are you serious? How did they find it? Okay. Well, I'm here. Everyone is on alert." He ended the call. He was so upset that he threw a chair against the wall.

"What's going on?" Amber asked.

"Someone just bombed the house in Scott, Arkansas. A few of our guys were killed. I tell you; we are in a fucking war."

Amber grabbed Andre by the arm and said, "Andre, I'm afraid. Why would someone do that?"

"They're after my family. Someone wants to kill us. Cassius White was killed at the mansion in Miami. His men think we had something to do with it. They're angry, and they are getting revenge by destroying our property and killing our people.

Amber asked, "What if they find us here? Why don't you call the police?"

"You don't get it, baby. In this business, we don't call the police. We handle it amongst ourselves. These men are extremely dangerous. But we won't be beaten. We'll kill every one of their men if we have to. Now, leave me alone. I have a few phone calls to make."

Andre made some calls and left to go to the larger cabin where Delgado was. He didn't come to the cabin that night. Amber was relieved. She took her phone out and called Cindy.

"Cindy, I'm scared. Andre said someone has blown up the house in Scott and killed a bunch of their workers. I'm afraid they'll find us here and come and do the same thing. I don't want to get caught up in the crossfire. I want to call the police to come and get me."

"Amber, stay right there. I'll be there in a couple of days to get you. Trust me. Just leave your phone on and act normal, and everything will be okay. Nobody's going to harm you if you listen to me."

"Okay, but I'm scared, cousin."

"I know you are, but trust me. I've got your back. Have I ever lied to you?"

"No, you haven't, but you said they're dangerous and..." Cindy interrupted her.

"Amber shut up, get off the damn phone, and wait. I'll be there to get you soon."

"Cindy, why are you whispering?"

149

"I have to go, Amber." The phone went dead. Amber was nervous. She got up to look out of the bedroom window. She walked out of the room. There, standing in the doorway, was Rita, who had a strange stare.

"Were you spying on me?" she asked Rita.

"No, I just came to see if you needed anything before I go to my cabin."

"Why would I need anything?"

"I'm just doing my job, ma'am."

"No, I don't need anything. You can go. Besides, it doesn't look like Andre will be back tonight; it's going on midnight."

"Well, I'll see you tomorrow."

Amber stood and watched as Rita walked away. She was suspicious of her behavior. She seemed to show up out of nowhere, easing around the cabin. She had the feeling she was watching her. Amber felt uneasy around her. She went back into the bedroom and tried to go to sleep. She tossed and turned with worry and fear the rest of the night. She finally dozed off.

The morning sun woke her. She squinted her eyes to adjust to the sunlight. She heard a sound on her right. She looked up and noticed Rita was unpacking her suitcase. She sprinted from her bed and snatched her things from her hands.

150

"Who told you to mess with my things?"

"Ma'am I'm unpacking your bags. It's a part of my duties. I unpack the guests when they come."

"I didn't ask you to unpack my things, and I don't want you to. Now go and do whatever it is you do around here but leave me alone."

"Would you like breakfast?"

"If I want breakfast, I'll ask for it; now please go!"

Rita left the room. Amber peeped to see if she was gone. She looked in her bag to see if her phone was still there. It was. She hid it in another bag. As she was doing so, Rita came back into the room unannounced, startling Amber.

"Do you ever knock around here or is barging in on people the way you do things? I could've been undressing."

"Mr. Delgado would like to speak with you, Ma'am."

"Thank you."

As Rita walked away, Amber mumbled under her breath, *"Knock the next time you come. Anybody knows when there's a closed door, the common courtesy is to knock before entering. I don't know where in the hell Andre got you from, but you are proving to be quite annoying."*

Amber walked from the bedroom into the living area. She saw the phone lying on the desk and picked it up.

"Darling, how are you this morning?" he asked.

"I'm doing okay. What happened to you last night? I was expecting you. I noticed you didn't come in."

"I was with my brother. We were out on business. I'll be there later this evening."

"I'll see you when you get here."

"Okay, my love." Amber went into the kitchen to pour her a glass of apple juice. She reached for a glass. Rita touched her hand, taking the glass from her.

"What can I get for you?" Rita asked.

"Nothing, I'm just pouring myself a glass of apple juice. Is that okay with you?"

"That's my job. I'll get it."

"Rita, or whatever your name is. I think I can pour a glass of juice. I'm not a complete idiot."

"But you do admit to being one, right?" Rita snarled.

152

"Nah bitch; I know you're not getting nasty with me!"

"I apologize. I couldn't resist," Rita said, looking at her and sizing Amber up to be a snobby prude.

"Let me ask you something Ms..... what's your name again?"

"My name is Amber."

"Amber, out of all of Mr. Delgado's house-whores I'd have to say you are the meanest thus far. What's your issue? Usually, women love having servants and workers to boss around."

"First of all, Rita, I'm not one of Andre's house-whores, and secondly, my parents were hard-working people before they retired. They worked all their lives to give me a better life. I wouldn't degrade them or their legacy by treating others poorly. Lastly, you've been snooping around, just popping up unannounced, and it's very annoying. To top it off, I caught you going through my things this morning. Of course, I got upset. I'm not used to that. I don't mean any harm, but you've been acting very creepy." Amber folded her arms and rolled her eyes her way. Rita snapped back at Amber,

"My job is to be as helpful as possible and stay out of the house guest's way. Mr. Delgado runs a tight ship around here and it's not nice to upset him. He does important work which sometimes keeps him on edge. He has entertained the world's most prominent people, and his staff has no way of knowing if the visitor plays an important part in the Delgado organization or not. As for me, I must treat all visitors as royalty. It's my duty to ensure complete comfort during his stay here. He's a powerful man and if one guest of Mr. Delgado complained, it could mean the difference between life or death. I know this personally because the last housekeeper didn't follow through with a house guest's demands, and let's just say; she's no longer with us."

Amber said, "I don't mind you doing your job, but I would like a little privacy so please knock before barging in. Ask me if I need help before you go through my things. I'm not that damn needy that I must have someone to unpack my underwear for me. I'm not used to that."

"I can respect that," Rita said.

"I apologize for being so moody, but I've been brought here basically against my will, and then I get here I'm told I'll be here indefinitely. I feel like a prisoner. I wasn't even asked if I wanted to come. I was just whisked away, and now that I'm here, I'm alone, and he gives me this horrible news and leaves me all to myself to worry. I was fine before he brought me here. Man, I should've stayed in law school, but nooo… not me. I've been making an ass of my life lately. Running around with the wrong people, now it's coming back to bite me in the ass, and I'm regretting every moment. It's just not worth it. Now *I'm* looking over *my* shoulder worried about what's going to happen next. I'm sitting here in a cabin in Timbuktu, and I'm stuck. I can't go anywhere. There are armed men all around us. I can't handle this."

Rita looked at her with a bit of sympathy and said, "Everything that glitters isn't always gold sweetheart. You young ladies love going after these rich men but when you pull the covers back, you get to see the truth for yourselves. Things aren't always so glamorous. Most women don't mind, but you don't seem to like it."

Amber said, "I thought Andre was a businessman. We were just having fun. He took me on trips and bought me nice things. I didn't think he would be on the run for his life putting me in the middle of it with him. I mean, what for? Nobody's looking for me; they're looking for him. I didn't sign up for all of this. What in the hell is going on around here?"

"Your questions have come too late, darling. You should've been asking those questions in the beginning. You're here now. You may as well make the best of it. Now can I get you something to eat?"

Amber nodded her head yes and sat back in her seat, staring into space. She was trying to evaluate things around her. Cindy was telling her to remain put. Rita was acting nonchalantly as if everything was practically normal. She wondered why Rita was not in a panic. She watched her as she did her work. She studied her demeanor. She watched as she walked around the kitchen as if she owned the place. Rita was an incredibly beautiful woman, and she didn't look like a maid in the least. Her appearance was more of a stunning female bodybuilder but not as masculine. Amber asked, "Rita, do you work out?"

"Why do you ask?"

"I ask because you're quite toned. I didn't know housekeeping put those types of muscles on a woman." As Rita talked, she continued working.

"Yes. I like looking good. I believe in watching what I eat and exercising." Out of curiosity, Amber asked,

"Has Andre ever tried to date you? I mean, you're gorgeous. If you let your hair down by taking it out of that ugly bun and then put on a little make-up, you would resemble a fashion model."

Rita, looking as if she was annoyed, said, "Although many men come on to me, I'm strictly professional, and I don't mix business with pleasure."

Reading a little more into what Rita was saying, Amber asked, "So you're saying it would be a pleasure to sleep with Andre?"

Rita immediately snapped back, "No, I'm not saying that. I'm saying I'm a professional at what I do and want to remain that way. I'm an employee of Mr. Delgado's. That's as far as our relationship goes. I'll leave it up to women like you to sleep with him. That's not my thing."

Amber said, "I'm not trying to insult you; I just know Andre loves women, and I find it hard to believe he would pass up someone as beautiful as you."

"Ms. Amber, real women can't be purchased with a few trinkets and random shopping sprees. Mr. Delgado respects that and values that in me. Now, if you're done talking, I have work to do. Breakfast will be ready in twenty minutes."

Amber watched her for a while as she prepared breakfast. She then went into the cabin's living quarters and sank into the sofa. Thinking about Cindy, she began to feel a bit anxious.

CHAPTER SIX

Jessica visited her friend, Detective Byron Armstrong, at the Little Rock Police Department. He was working on several cases. She was interested in the Delgado brothers. She checked in at the front desk. She proceeded to Armstrong's office. He was on his computer looking up information on some of his cases. She popped her head in and lightly knocked at his already-opened door.

"What 'cha working on Armstrong?" He looked up from his computer.

"Hey there, Barnes. I'm working on a cold case. It seems we got a hit on a DNA profile of that murder of the store clerk over on Woodrow Street. I'm gathering all the evidence so that we can obtain a warrant. What's up with you? What're you working on over there at the agency?" Jessica walked into his office and took a seat.

"Nothing that I need the police's help with yet. I'm here because I want to know what's happening with the Delgado brothers."

"Well, what about them?" he asked. Jessica told him all that Blaine shared with her about Delgado.

"We're still working on the case of Cindy's employees. We feel that Delgado had something to do with the murders, but we don't have any evidence to prove it, and without proof, we have nothing to charge him with. I tell you; this guy operates like a ghost.

His dirty work is done, but there are never any witnesses or evidence pointing to him or anybody else."

Jessica asked, "What about him going by Cindy's place and threatening her niece? Can anything be done about that?" Detective Armstrong responded.

"Again, no evidence. Delgado's not a fool. He didn't last this long by being one. He's skilled at the game. The FBI is investigating him, and they can't seem to find anything on him. All his businesses seem to be legit. The Internal Revenue Service has gone over his finances with a fine-tooth comb. As far as I know, we have nothing on this man. We know he's guilty as sin, but that little thing called evidence is missing. Until then, we have no case." Jessica had a frown on her face.

"Nobody's that lucky for this long. He's going to slip up soon, and when he does, it's going to come down on him like Armageddon." Armstrong looked at her with a slight grin on his face.

"Funny you should mention that. Haven't you heard the news, Jessica?"

"What news?"

"You're right. Nobody's that lucky. His mansion in Scott was blown to bits. On top of that, I heard that his estate over in

159

Miami was attacked. Someone killed this known drug lord named Cassius White on his property. After that killing, Delgado left Miami. He hasn't contacted the police about his home that was destroyed over in Scott. The Delgado brothers may be already dead. I highly doubt it, but nobody's heard from either of them. Some are thinking their bodies could be among those at the scene. Several of his men were killed. Forensics guys are still on the scene." Jessica said, "Why am I just now hearing about this?" "It's all over the news and the internet." Why aren't you working on that case?"

"Because the FBI has taken over that investigation, and that's out of my jurisdiction. You already know that. That's going to be on Pulaski County and North Little Rock., The only crime I'm allowed to work on is the one with Angelica, who was found on Chicot Road; I'm sure they'll eventually take over that case as well, especially since these cases may tie in together. If I hear something, I'll let you know." Jessica was excited to hear the news about Delgado. She was curious and wanted to know more.

"I'm going to ride by Delgado's place and be nosey. Also, I will contact Amy Stokes, who works at the bureau. I'll see what she can tell me."

"Okay, but they're tight-lipped on this one. Good luck."

"Thanks, I'll check with you later."

Jessica left the police department. She looked up her friend Amy Stokes at the Bureau. She wasn't in, so she left a message for her. She drove by the Delgado place in Scott. She looked at the destruction. It looked as if a bomb had hit it. There was hardly anything left of the place. It was still smoldering. The fire department kept a steady stream of water on it. The once glamorous mansion was reduced to rubble. *"Wow, what a lovely mess. Delgado has really pissed somebody off this time."* What she didn't know was that Cindy had been there. Cindy killed as many of the outside guards as she could; afterward, she set off a few grenades, killing everyone on site. She left no survivors. The more Cindy killed, the easier killing became for her. She was in vigilante mode, and she would not stop until everyone in the Delgado camp was dead. Jessica surveyed the damages from a distance. The place was cordoned off. The media was camped out. It began to rain, so Jessica left. She called Blaine to discuss what she'd learned. Blaine didn't know about the incident at the Delgado mansion. He'd spent the night at Cindy's home. Cindy came in around one in the morning, and they both slept in. Blaine woke Cindy, who was lying in his arms. He had to shake her because she was sound asleep.

"Cindy babe, wake up for a minute. I have something I want to tell you." Cindy finally opened her eyes. She looked at him.

"What is it, babe?"

"Jessie just called. She told me to watch the morning news."

"Watch the morning news for what?"

"She said someone attacked Delgado's place in Scott, and they think he may be dead." Cindy was emotionless.

She looked at Blaine and asked, "What if he's not dead?"

Blaine was concerned about Amber and asked, "Babe, was your cousin Amber still with them? She may have been in there too. No, Amber is not with him, Honey. She's out of town with friends. She had an audition. She's fine. She's going to call me later."

"Can you verify that?"

"Trust me, Amber is okay," she said.

Cindy lay on Blaine's chest and went back to sleep. Blaine wondered why Cindy didn't react to hearing about the explosion. He was curious, so he watched the news himself. After getting another hour of sleep, Cindy got up and got dressed. Blaine went to work.

Jessica called Cindy to discuss the case, but Cindy told her she was too busy to chat and to call her another time. She left Amber a text message to call her. Much to her surprise, Amber quickly called her back.,

"Yes Cindy"

"Listen to what I'm going to tell you. I've found your location. I know exactly where you are. Now, do me a favor. Open your cell phone when we end this call. Look inside, and you'll find a tracking device. I placed it on your phone to keep up with you just in case something like this happened. When you see Andre, put the device somewhere on him or in something he will definitely carry with him, preferably in his phone. After that, do nothing. Just wait for me. Don't call your parents, and don't call the police or anybody; you just wait for me to call you. Can you charge your phone?"

"Yes, I can."

"Do that, and I'll be there in less than two days. I'll call you with instructions."

"Okay Cousin, hurry though."

"Get off the phone sweetie."

"I love you, Cindy."

"You can tell me you love me when you see me."

They ended the call. Amber did as Cindy told her. She took the tracking device and held on to it until Andre came to the cabin later that evening. Rita fixed a large meal. Andre was tired from being up the previous night. He drank plenty of liquor, and he and Amber went to the bedroom.

Amber was on her game. She showered and went to the bedroom with nothing on but a thong. He admired her cute firm little ass. She flirted with him. She climbed atop him and played with him, doing everything to make him happy. Wetting her fingers with saliva, she reached behind and pulled his member slowly and methodically, massaging it while rubbing it against her butthole. She slid down on his erect penis and threw her head back in pleasure. He looked up at the smile on her beautiful, youthful face and full, long blonde hair. He groped her firm breast with stiffened nipples large and pink. He was mesmerized as she rode him. He watched as her tiny little ass slid down on his erect penis. She knew what he liked and gave in to his every whim. On the edge of ecstasy, he whispered,

"Amber, sweetheart, I love you. I know I've been acting strange lately. I apologize darling; I'm not sure how much longer I have to live. That's why I want you to have my child. I want a son to carry on my name. If anything ever happened to me, you'll have my child and my money. Through your womb, I want you to fulfill my legacy." She slowed her rhythm and asked,

"But why me, Andre? What makes me so different from all the others?"

"Amber, you're full of life. You're smart, beautiful, and one fantastic young lady. There's more to you than you know. People are puzzled by my choice to love you. I know they think you're just another woman, but to me, you're everything. You don't know what

I've been through over the past few years, but meeting and loving you has given me new life."

Andre was showing a bit of humanity. Amber was almost touched hearing him speak of her positively, but as he spoke, she heard Cindy's voice playing in her head. She knew she had to make this the performance of her life. She made passionate love to Andre.

"Andre darling, I love you. I want you. Give me all of you. Give me your seed. I want to have your babies. I'll willingly give you my body to carry your child. It's my pleasure," she said as she rode him with perfect rhythm. His hands were on her waist, pulling her down on him as she lifted her body. She tilted her head back and screamed his name. "Andre baby, I love you." He couldn't hold back any longer. He was coming to a climax. After sex, Amber lay on top of him. His penis was still inside her. She was panicking inside because she didn't want to become pregnant, but she knew she had to remain still. She had no access to the morning-after pill. She brought no feminine hygiene products with her. She was highly at risk of becoming pregnant. Andre was so turned on by her, that he made love to her for a couple of more hours. Drunk and extremely exhausted, he went to sleep.

She took the tracking device from her phone and carefully placed it into his cell phone, as Cindy requested. She used the restroom and lay beside him, hoping Cindy would come through. She lay there thinking about it throughout the night.

The following morning, when Andre awoke, Amber again had sex with him. They showered together, and she spent some loving playtime with him until it was time for him to leave. He was in a better mood. She followed him as he walked to the door, kissed him, and told him she couldn't wait for him to return. After he was gone, she showered again. After she showered, she got dressed and waited as Cindy instructed her. Rita went about the cabin doing what she normally does.

As time went on, Amber began to worry. It was finally nightfall, and she hadn't heard from Cindy or Andre. She was going into panic mode. While she paced back and forth, Rita came in and announced she was leaving for the night. Amber was almost afraid to be alone and was tempted to ask Rita to stay, but she didn't. She sat still until she finally fell asleep on the sofa. The vibrations of her phone awakened her. She looked at it, and it was a text message from Cindy telling her to call. She called her immediately.

"Yes Cindy"

"I'll be there tomorrow to get you."

"Okay, so what're you going to do, knock on the door and get me? There are armed men everywhere."

"I'll be there tomorrow; be ready."

"Okay."

As they were talking, Rita, Delgado, and a few of his men barged into the cabin. Delgado looked at Amber. His eyes were almost swollen shut, and his hair was disheveled. He wasn't the usual handsome, suave man who commanded attention. His face was red, and he had a look of pain combined with anger. He took her cell phone from her, trying to see whom she'd been conversing with. Cindy heard Delgado's voice and knew Amber was in immediate danger. She wasn't counting on that, but she wasn't blinded by it. Cindy didn't say anything to him. He continued to try to get her to talk. She listened in the background. He grabbed Amber by the hair.

"Who were you talking to on the phone?" Amber was afraid to tell him.

"Nobody Anton."

"Bitch you're lying to me, now tell me who was on the fucking phone?"

"It was nobody; just my family."

"Who did you reveal our location to?" Amber began to cry.

"Nobody I swear. I don't even know where I am. I couldn't tell you how to get here or how to leave from here." Delgado instructed Rita, now dressed in a black suit resembling a female

167

secret service agent, to take Amber and bring her with them. Delgado searched Amber's bags. Rita pointed a gun at Amber and said, "Let's go little Ms. Prissy." Amber was afraid and confused. She was taken to the larger cabin and held there. She could hear everyone talking in the background. Delgado was terribly upset. Looking closer at his face, he appeared to have been crying. She overheard them talking about Andre. She asked Rita, who was watching her for Delgado, what was going on.

"Well, Mr. Andre Delgado was killed earlier tonight along with another one of our guards. They think it may have something to do with you. Nobody knows we're here, but I told them I overheard you talking on the phone, so they feel their hide-out has been compromised. Mr. Delgado was killed just a couple of miles away out on the highway." Amber had a somber expression on her face.

"Andre has been killed?

She balled herself into a knot and began to cry.

"Oh my god, how was he killed?"

"The car he was riding in was riddled with bullets, and afterward, it exploded."

"Are you sure he's dead?" Amber asked.

"Yes, I'm sure. Why do you think you're here? Mr. Delgado wants to know who you spoke with."

168

"I only talked with my family. Nobody else. I swear."

"Are you sure?"

"Yes, just family. What's going to happen to me?" Amber asked.

"Nothing; if everything checks out, we'll have one of our men take you home."

"So, I'm not free to go home now? I didn't kill Andre; I cared about him. Please have someone take me home. Tell Anton I want to go. I'll tell him if you won't."

"Amber, please, don't do this. You could end up seriously hurt. Now I suggest you keep your mouth shut for the time being."

Cindy called Amber's phone. Delgado answered as she suspected he would. "May I speak to Amber please?"

"Who's calling?"

"Tell her it's Cindy."

Delgado said, "Cindy, this is Anton. I have your cousin's phone. My brother has been killed and we're trying to figure out who's responsible for his death."

"I hate hearing about your brother. I send my condolences to your mother, but I would like to speak with Amber please."

169

Delgado told Cindy, "You know what; I'm not ready for her to speak with anybody yet. Why are you calling?"

"I didn't think I needed your permission to talk to my own family, but since you asked, I'm calling because I'm concerned about her. She and I were talking earlier, and our call was dropped. I just want to know if she's okay."

"Why wouldn't she be?"

"Well, your not-so-subtle threat to do bodily harm to her comes to mind, and besides, you're answering her phone, which causes me to be alarmed."

Delgado called for Rita. He handed her the phone. She pressed the speaker button so they could hear the conversation between the two women.

"Hey cousin."

"Hello Amber. I'm sorry, but our call dropped. Is everything okay?"

"I'm okay, but someone killed Andre." Amber began to cry.

"I'm so sorry cousin. I know it hurts. I know how much you loved him, and he loved you too."

"Yes, he did. We were going to have a family, but he's gone now."

"Are you going to be okay?" Cindy asked.

"Yes, I'm here with Anton."

"Would you like for me to come and pick you up?" Delgado was listening, and Cindy knew it. Looking towards Amber, he shook his head.

"No Cindy, Anton is going to bring me home soon. I'm going to stay here for now. I love you. Tell Mom I'll call her when I get settled."

"Okay Hun, try and take care of yourself. Again, I'm sorry for your loss."

"Thank you, Cindy."

They ended the call. Rita handed the phone back to Delgado. Convinced by Cindy's little acting skit, he motioned for her to give the phone back to Amber. He knew he would be held accountable if anything happened to Amber. Besides, she was the least of his worries. After hearing their call, he reasoned that it was Cash's men who'd killed his brother. Besides, he felt Cindy wasn't intelligent enough to pull off such a hit. His hunter was closing in on him and he felt it. He began to make plans to leave the cabin immediately. In the meantime, Cindy had to lay low in the area because the police were swarming the place.

Not only did she want her cousin home safe, she wanted Delgado dead, but she had to wait for the perfect timing. It looked as if it would be after Andre's funeral. If she had her way, it would be a double funeral.

Cindy had been down on the old highway. She followed the tracking device that Amber planted on Andre. She parked on vacant property and waited for the dark-colored SUV to come down the road. As the headlights approached, she hid behind a large tree. Once the vehicle was in full view, she began firing on the occupants inside. She homed in on Andre, killing him and then the driver. The car came to a halt in a nearby ditch. She continued firing on the vehicle, hitting the tank and bursting into flames. After throwing one of her grenades, she ran back to her vehicle, got inside, and left.

Jessica heard about the death of Andre Delgado. She tried her friend Amy Stokes at the bureau who finally returned her call.

"Hi Amy, this is Jessica Barnes here."

"Jessica, long time no see. I haven't heard from you in ages. How're things going with you?

"I can't complain. Ever since we solved that last case, we've been busier than ever. Also, I found out my dad was sick, and I took some time away to care for him. Doctors say he's gonna be okay so I'm back at it for now."

"Jessica, I'm sorry I couldn't make it to your last dinner party. I've been on assignment for a while now. Actually, I'm still on assignment. I came in this week for a debriefing, but I must return to the field. I'm working on a major case, and we're almost done. I received your message to call you. What's going on?"

Jessica told her everything about Cindy's situation. Afterward, she asked, "Have you heard anything about what's happening with this particular case?"

"Jessica, as much as I would like to help you, you know I can't comment much on ongoing investigations. But I can tell you this: from what I hear, whoever is killing off these guys is killing everyone the bureau's been watching for years. A few guys are coming forward out of fear asking for the government's protection. They're close to breaking the Delgado code of silence. Just as we were about to begin indictments on some within the organization, it was discovered that they'd been killed. It appears they're in some sort of war. We've had to pull some of our men for safety's sake. Whoever is doing this is quite skilled. We think they're a group from Cuba who'll give their very lives for Cassius White. We can't seem to catch them, and we never know when they're going to strike. They know exactly where to hit. Perhaps it's an inside job and someone Anton Delgado knows personally must be setting him up. I mean how they knew about the place on the other side of

Russellville is beyond us. It's extremely secluded and they're hardly ever at that place. They didn't attack the home, but they managed to kill the brother. I want to know why they didn't just kill everyone inside the home. But I'm saying too much, and I don't want to jeopardize the investigation."

Amy trusted Jessica. That's why she threw her a few nuggets on the case. She knew with Jessica working things in an unofficial capacity, she was bound to find something useful.

"I understand Amy. I want to know what's being done about my friend Cindy. She's on edge because of the deaths of her employees. She closed her business because of threats from Delgado."

Agent Stokes said, "Hell from the looks of things, she'll be okay because somebody's out to get him. Jessica, I must go back to work now."

"Okay Amy, thanks for returning my call. We'll chat soon" Jessica ended the call.

Cindy was confident that Delgado would allow Amber to come home. Although she was responsible for Andre's death, she knew Delgado didn't know so it was only a matter of time before Amber would be released. If he released her too soon, she could possibly lose him forever. She wanted to go in with guns blazing but that would put Amber in danger.

Jessica called Cindy. She was adamant that she meets with her. Cindy agreed, so she went by the agency. "Jessica, what do you want to see me about?"

"I want to know how you've been doing."

"I'm making it."

"How are you since the closing of your club?"

"I've been doing as well as can be expected under the circumstances."

"When do you think you'll open again? I know that place is your life, and it's become a staple in the community. We miss it being open, but I can understand your concerns."

"Jessica, I had to close for the safety of my employees. Since a few of them quit and two were murdered, there was no need to put anyone else's life in jeopardy, so closing seemed like the right thing to do."

"We can get protection for your place Cindy."

"I don't think so. You don't know Anton. He won't go away; besides; who'll protect my employees once they leave the club? Remember, neither of them were killed at the club but close to their homes. Their murders still remain unsolved. Perhaps he'll get what's coming to him soon."

"It seems as if it's already happening. He's being hunted and everyone around him is being killed. His place was destroyed in Miami, and he lost all of his men there due to an explosion and the same thing happened to his home in Scott. He lost many men there. I hear it's because this drug lord was killed in Miami. To top all of that off, his brother was killed last night. It looks like he underestimated his opponent. I bet he didn't know they would come after him as vicious as they have. It must be an army of guys after him. The feds love it because they think it'll drive Delgado to them for protection, but I say in doing so he'll only sign his death warrant. I think whoever is killing off his people is an inside job."

"So, who do the police think are doing it?"

"They say it's Cash's men from Columbia. You know they won't stop killing until everyone is dead. Since his brother is dead it looks as if he's next."

"So, they think a group of men from Columbia is doing this?" Cindy asked. "Girl with as much firepower as they're using, yeah, it's somebody powerful doing these killings, and they know when to strike, and they keep getting away with it, leaving no evidence behind."

"Wow, that's amazing," Cindy said looking sneaky.

Jessica asked her, "How do you feel about all of this happening? You must get a sense of satisfaction knowing that he's getting his just dues."

"Jessie, if you live that lifestyle and you hurt innocent people, it's bound to catch up with you one day. You can't fuck over people and get away with it."

"You're right about that. I guess we can sit back and wait and see what's going to happen next. So how is your cousin Amber doing?"

"Amber is doing fine. She is upset about his death, but she is going to be okay."

"So, is she going to be staying with you?"

"She's in a safe place for now. I really don't want to discuss this anymore Jessica."

"Cindy, you're my friend, and I want to help as much as I can. I want to give you my support. I don't want you to have to go through this alone. Blaine tells me he's worried about you and so am I."

"Jessica, I know you care about us. I thank you for your kindness towards me all these years. There are times in life we go through horrible things, and we have to weather them alone. I don't

177

wish to involve you or Blaine in this madness I'm going through. I must sort things out on my own. I just need to know that when all is said and done, you'll still be here for me and that you'll keep me in your prayers. No matter what happens to me, I want you to know I love you and Blaine."

"Cindy, you're talking like you're going to die or something. I know you're worried about Delgado harming you. We're not about the let that happen."

"Neither am I," Cindy snapped sharply. She was about to say more, then she realized she would incriminate herself. She knew not to mention too much around Jessica. She couldn't afford for her to catch on to her, not when she was so close to killing Delgado. She wouldn't even allow anyone to know that Amber was still in Delgado's home.

"Wow, you said that with confidence," Jessica said surprised.

"I'm confident that Anton will get what he has coming to him soon enough."

"I just wanted to make sure you were okay and to let you know I'm here if you need me."

"Thank you, Jessica." Jessica stood to her feet and so did Cindy. She hugged her."

"I have to get going," Cindy said.

"Take care of yourself."

"I will Jessie." Cindy went to see Blaine and let him know she was leaving. Jessica sat staring out the window and thinking about Cindy. She desperately wanted to help her friend, but Cindy was shutting her out which was unlike her. They'd managed to work together for years, and Cindy had always been cooperative with her but not now, she'd totally shut down.

Unbeknownst to Cindy, Jessica decided she would watch out for her to help protect her. She informed Blaine, who agreed to it, especially if he wasn't around. They were going to keep their eyes and ears open to ensure her safety.

Cindy didn't know she was being followed by Jessica. She went on with her plan to kill Delgado. She got with Big Dan and got more weapons. She continued hatching a plan to get close to Delgado. Since he was already vulnerable, she decided to play on it. She called him to talk. Delgado answered the phone. She could tell by his voice that he was in distress.

"Hello, Anton."

"Hello, Cindy."

"I'm calling to check on you. How are you holding up?"

"Cindy darling, you don't have to pretend to care about me. Especially considering the things I've said and done to hurt you."

"Anton if I didn't care to some degree, I wouldn't be calling you. We've had our differences in the past and I did love you once. Is it so hard for you to believe that? I want to know how you're doing. I know how much your brother meant to you. You guys were close. I can only imagine the pain you're going through right now."

As they were talking, she was toying around with her pistol. She wasn't feeling sympathy for him in the least. It was all she could do to keep from bragging about the kills. She so desperately wanted to ask him how it feels to lose someone he loves. As many lives as he has affected for his own selfish gain, she found it excruciating to even get in a kind word without cursing him. She was thinking about her baby boy and her friends. She almost began to crack but she held herself together. She took the advice she'd given to Amber. She was in a role of her life.

"It truly hurts. My dear mother is devastated." Cindy was pleased to hear of his pain.

"When will the memorial service be? I would love to pay my respects. I want to support you and Amber. Andre was her love, and they truly adored each other."

"Yes, much to my dismay, he did care for her."

Delgado wasn't thinking clearly. He was weakened by all that had happened. He believed Cindy when she told him she was sincere about her caring for him. He let his guard down and opened up to her. She pretended to listen as he poured out his heart.

Delgado would play God in so many lives, deciding who would live or die, but now he was reduced to a mere mortal. He was feeling horrible. His brother was gone, and his empire had all but crumbled. His men were afraid and most began to abandon him. She pretended to care knowing all along she was plotting his death. After about an hour of talking, he was putty in her hands. Like the pied piper, she intended on playing him eventually luring him to his death.

Soon after their talk, Amber called. She told Cindy that Delgado was sending one of his men to take her home and she was going to the apartment Andre purchased for her. Once she made it home, she called Cindy, and she immediately went over to see her. Cindy was at the door. Amber hurried and opened it. She fell into Cindy's arms and cried.

"Cindy I was so afraid. It was horrible. I thought I would never make it out of there alive. What did you say to Anton to get him to let me go?"

"Anton isn't stupid sweetie. I knew you were there. For him to hurt you would've meant he had to answer for it, and he didn't want those problems."

"Oh my god, I'm so glad to be away from there. There are armed men everywhere. They held me at gunpoint and took me to the main cabin and kept me there until you called him. It was then he decided to release me. Someone killed Andre Cindy. I know I was planning on leaving him, but to know that he's dead is painful. I feel relieved to be out of there, but I feel a sense of sadness that he is gone."

"Trust me, honey, if he hadn't been killed, they wouldn't have hesitated to kill you." Amber was emotional. She thought about all the fun times she had with Andre, and she began to cry. "I just can't believe he's dead."

"Amber, can you tell me how many men you saw around there? How is the layout of the home?"

"He has about seven or eight guys in the main cabin and around two for the other two homes. One of the security personnel is a lady named Rita. She was pretending to be a maid but when Andre was killed, she was dressed as one of the other guys. She's the one who held me at gunpoint. They're no longer staying there. Anton and his men left as I was leaving. I heard him saying he was taking a helicopter somewhere."

Cindy continued to question Amber about her stay. She seemed to be taking the death of Andre awfully hard. Amber refused to leave her apartment, so Cindy stayed with her until she requested some time to herself. Cindy left her alone and went home. She was able to rest for a while knowing Amber was safe.

CHAPTER SEVEN

It had been a month since the death of Andre, and Cindy was still playing the role of a supportive friend to Delgado. Although she didn't know where his new hide-out was, she was in constant contact with him. She was at her home getting plans together for possibly opening the club while she was planning her attack within the coming month. Her doorbell rang. It was Amber. She rushed in when Cindy opened the door.

"Amber, what's going on?" Amber, looking nervous, said, "I need to talk to you. It's important."

"Come inside." Amber was seated.

"What's going on?"

"Cindy, I'm pregnant!" Amber blurted out. Cindy looked at her in disbelief. "You're what?" Amber looked a bit excited but nervous. "I said I'm pregnant."

"What? You can't be."

"Yes, but I am." Amber almost beamed with pride. Stunned at the news, Cindy was speechless. She noticed the slight smile on Amber's face. Her facial expression let her know that she was excited about the pregnancy, and this disappointed her. Amber continued speaking. "I took a pregnancy test; well, actually, I took two of them, and they both were positive. I was feeling ill, and I missed my period. I went to the doctor, and they confirmed I was pregnant."

"So, what are you going to do about it?" Cindy asked. Amber lowered her head a little and whispered,

"I was thinking about keeping the baby."

Although Cindy was distraught over the news, she didn't want to say the wrong thing. She wondered, *"How could she possibly think of keeping this baby after all that family put us through?"* She was trying to eliminate the Delgado name from the earth, and her cousin had one growing inside her. Cindy took a seat.

"What's wrong, cousin?"

"Amber, are you seriously thinking about keeping the baby of a known gangster?" Amber looked a bit stunned and replied,

"Yes, I plan on keeping my baby. I'm not a gangster. This child can't help who its father was. He's dead now and I like the thought of having my baby."

"But Amber, are you even ready to take care of a baby? You'll be a single mother, and you don't even have a career. How are you going to be able to afford to take care of a child?"

"Cindy, I'll make it. Besides, I have a little money saved up that Andre gave me. It's not much but it'll give me a nice head start until I figure out what I'm going to do. Also, he put both of those condos in my name, the one in Miami and the one here in Little Rock. I'm going to put them both up for sale, buy myself a small, affordable home, and get ready for my baby's arrival. Cindy, there are women who have it worse than I do who are making it. I know I can make it too. I'm going to get my law degree, and I'll get a job or possibly even open my own practice one day. My parents worked hard to pay for it, and I've been given a second chance at life. I promised myself that if I ever got out of that situation, I would go back and finish school. You may not approve of me having Andre's baby, and I understand your concern. My baby's father is dead. This baby may have Delgado blood, but it doesn't have to live like one. I can teach it a better way. My baby is a part of me, and I don't want to kill my child."

Cindy was not impressed with the news, but she had to set aside her hatred for the Delgados to accept her cousin's decision.

"I can't do anything about your decision. I just hope you make the right one that's best for you."

Amber, hoping to persuade her to see things from her perspective asked,

"Cindy, why does my child have to die for something its father has done? Andre may have been a bad man, but that doesn't

186

mean my baby will turn out to be the same as its ancestors. What if someone felt that you didn't deserve to live for something your parents did? You're not them. This baby will have a part of our family in it. I plan on planting all the positive seeds that we have in us, my parents, and our ancestors. With the proper love and guidance, this baby will grow up the right way. Now, what do you say Cousin Cindy?" She took both Cindy's hands and placed them on her belly.

"This is your little cousin in here. Can you show this baby the love you've always shown me?"

Cindy managed to put a smile on her face. She hugged Amber. "Since you put it that way. then yes. I'm happy for you." Cindy was happy to hear Amber speak of her child in the way she did. She began to think of her own son. She began to see how insensitive her actions were. She was suggesting that Amber kill her child who was a part of her. It was an unreasonable request to ask of any mother. Cindy thought Amber was right. Why did her child have to die because of his family? Although the child would live, Cindy was sure that his uncle was going to die. She and Amber talked more on the subject and after a while of visiting, Amber went back to her apartment.

Cindy didn't want Delgado to learn about the pregnancy. It would be one more thing for him to try and control. Since his brother was dead, he would definitely want to take the child and raise it as

187

his own. He didn't have any children. He managed to get Cindy pregnant, and she miscarried. She felt it was due to all the fighting they were doing. But after the death of her son Micah, she wasn't ready to have any more children. Thinking of her own son, she was ready to put her plan into motion. She beefed up her calls to Delgado. It was during one of her phone calls that he informed her that his attorney needed to speak with Amber.

"What does he need to speak with Amber about?" Cindy asked.

"My brother left a will and in it, he seems to have left Amber something. Normally, I wouldn't allow this sort of thing, and I would have it taken care of immediately. Cindy knew exactly what he meant by that. He continued speaking.

"I don't like it when outside women want to take a part of what we've built here. But my brother, God rest his soul, was in love with this girl and she brought him much joy. So much so, that he was thinking of her before he died. I want to fulfill my brother's wishes by giving her what he wanted her to have. It's the last thing I can do for him."

"Anton, are you serious? You plan on actually giving Amber what your brother has left for her?" "Yes, I do." She was surprised at the notion.

"Well, I'd like to know what brought about this change."

"Trust me, my love, it's only out of my love for my brother. I don't know your cousin all that well, but I saw how happy she made my brother. I could only think that when he died perhaps, he was thinking of her. My brother was my life. It was only me, him, and my mama after our father was killed. I took care of him. I watched out for him. I don't see how I'm going to make it without him. My mama is devastated. Life has gone out of her. His death has really shaken us up. I loved my brother, and I owe it to him to obey his last will, even if it means giving a portion of what he has to your cousin. So please inform her."

Cindy hesitated. She held the phone in her hand. She knew telling Amber what Delgado was saying wasn't a good idea, but it was only a matter of time before he found her anyway so she would tell her. She let out a sigh and said,

"I'll let her know."

"Thank you, darling." Cindy used this opportunity to try and get a little closer to Delgado.

"Anton, what's going on with you?"

"I'm trying to cope day by day?"

Pretending to care Cindy said, "I would love to come and see you soon. Perhaps I can come over and sit with you for a while. I wanted to come sooner, but I thought I'd allow things to die down a little. Would you like for me to come and visit you?"

Delgado answered quickly, "Cindy, let me get back to you on that. I'm kinda laying low for a while. I can call you one day soon and perhaps we can meet. I must watch my surroundings. There's someone out to kill me. They got my brother, but I have to make sure to stay on the safe side until my men can catch whoever is doing this."

"Surely you don't think I'm a vicious killer do you, Anton?"

"No, I don't, but someone is out to get me, and I have to be very careful. I'll call you soon and I'll have a car come for you and bring you to where I am."

"That sounds great. I'll be looking forward to your call." Cindy ended the call and said to herself, *"Keep your friends close and your enemies closer."*

Cindy's plan of gaining his trust was working. After ending the call, she contacted Amber. She told her what Delgado said, and she urged her not to take any money from the family. She also urged her not to tell him about the pregnancy. Amber was excited to know that Andre thought of her enough to leave her something. She wanted the money. She needed it to care for her child and she felt it was due to her. Again, she ignored her cousin's sound advice. She contacted the attorney involved. He met with her, and she and he sat in his office with Delgado on video conferencing. She sat on the other side of the conference table looking at Delgado and waiting for the attorney to tell her what she was getting. The attorney looked as if he had nothing to do with the crime syndicate. He was a corporate attorney, and he was strikingly handsome. Not at all like what she thought he would be. He was professional. His name is Santiago Burkett.

"Ms. Amber Brooks. You are here today for the reading of the last will of Mr. Andre Eduardo Delgado. Mr. Anton Delgado and my secretary are here as witnesses to the reading of this will. Anton nodded his head. The attorney read the will aloud. There were items left to his mother. The will went on for several pages. When he got to the part that pertained to Amber, she sat upright.

"And to my darling Amber, what can I say of the great joys you have brought me? He continued to read what he was leaving to her. Then he came to a stipulation clause that stated she would get even more if she had children. She was all too delighted to see how significant the amount had changed if children were involved. After hearing that she blurted out,

"I'm pregnant with his child" Stunned by the news, the attorney looked at her and asked, "You're pregnant?"

She smiled at him.

"Yes, I am." Anton looked at Amber on the monitor. You're pregnant with my brother's child?" She looked up at the screen and said,

"Yes, he wanted me to have his child. We're going to have a baby." Anton was elated. He looked at Amber a little closer and said,

"A part of my brother will live on." Although Amber felt she was doing the right thing by gaining a future for her child, she unknowingly opened the door for Delgado to control her life and everything about the baby. He initially was going to allow her to have the money and split, but not now. He felt she owed it to him to allow him to be a part of the pregnancy and the child's life when born. Once it was determined by Delgado and his attorney that Amber was indeed telling the truth about the pregnancy, Delgado hired the best doctors and nurses to care for Amber.

Two weeks had passed, and Cindy decided to visit Amber. There was a doctor there checking her vitals. The doctor placed his stethoscope in his bag. "Well Ms. Brooks, it looks like everything is okay." I'll be back in two weeks." The doctor got his things, spoke to Cindy, and left. Cindy looked around and noticed a lot of expensive baby items. There were a few things set up in the spare bedroom that resembled a small clinic. There was even an ultrasound machine in there. She had a housekeeper and a cook, and she also had a female guard watching her home.

"Amber, what in the world is going on here?"

"Oh, it's nothing; I just got a little help."

"How can you afford to have all of these people working for you?"

"They don't work for me. Anton hired them to look after me."

"Oh my god, Amber! Did you tell Anton about the baby? How could you?"

"I had no choice. As they were reading the will, it specifically stipulated what was to happen if I were pregnant or if I had children. I had to tell the attorney I was pregnant."

"No, you didn't Amber. You were going to get the money anyway. Do you know what this means? You are now a part of that family, and you'll never be safe. Delgado will take your baby from you and hire others to raise it, is that what you want?"

"No, he won't do that."

"Girl, you better wake your ass up. When will you learn? You just sold your baby into a life of crime. Do you actually think Anton is going to let you go that easy? Aside from Anton, there are no more Delgado men. If this baby is a boy, you will lose him forever. How could you be so stupid?" Cindy was irate. She was even more ready to kill Delgado.

She stormed out of Amber's place. She got in her car and, out of anger and frustration, screamed at the top of her lungs,

"I hate this motherfucker!!! It seems like he will never leave my life, but that's some bullshit. I'm going to stop playing games with this motherfucker. I'm going to find him and kill him myself. I don't give a damn if I have to go to prison."

She sped out of the parking lot. She didn't see a car coming from the side. …. Bam! The car collided with her T-boning her vehicle. Cindy was trapped inside the vehicle. The other vehicle's occupant tried to help her out, but the door was stuck. The police and paramedics arrived. So did Jessica. She stood by as Cindy was removed from the vehicle. Cindy was lying on the stretcher, looking up at Jessica. Jessica held her hand. "You're going to be okay, Cindy," she said.

"Jessica, how did you know I was here? How did you get here so soon?"

"I was in the area. I heard the crash, and I came to help. To my surprise, it was your car. I'll meet you at the hospital. I've already called Blaine."

Jessica didn't want to tell Cindy that she had been watching her to protect her. That's why she was on the scene of the accident so soon. Cindy was taken to the hospital. She was kept overnight for observation. She had a mild concussion and a bump on the side of her head. She sat in her hospital bed reflecting on her accident and what caused her to be so off-focus that she almost got herself and an innocent guy killed.

She was losing it. She knew she had to focus, so she decided to calm down for a while. Her obsession with killing her target was getting the best of her, and she was afraid she would begin to make mistakes. Blaine rushed into the room.

"Cindy baby, are you okay?" he asked, rushing to her side.

"Yes Blaine, I'm okay. I got a little bump, but it's nothing to get excited about."

"Jessica told me that she saw you leaving Amber's place and she saw the collision. She said you seemed upset before the accident."

"What do you mean? She told me she just happened to be in the area, and she heard the collision. How did she know I was upset? Was she following me?"

"Baby, calm down." She was looking at him, wanting answers.

"Yes, she was following you. She's just trying to protect you. We love you, babe. There's been a lot of violence lately with the death of your employees and your need to close the club. Let's not mention the latest issues with Delgado and the death of his brother. We want to make sure you're okay. Baby, you've been going through so much lately. You've lost people you care about, and I know it's affecting you. You cry in my arms at night. You won't talk to me, but I know you're hurting. It hurts me to see you this way, and it seems as if there is nothing I can do to help."

Cindy's anger subsided. She knew they meant well. "Baby, I'm so sorry. I've been going through a lot. I didn't mean to shut you out. I don't want to burden you with my problems. You have your children to think about. I don't want to be a distraction to you and the boys. What I'm going through, you can't help me with anyway. Besides, having you there to hold me every night is plenty enough. Just because I don't discuss my issues with you, doesn't mean you aren't helping me. Your presence is therapeutic. How do you think I've made it this far? Just keep on loving me like you're doing. Don't change on me. That's all the help I need. I know how to handle Anton."

"Baby, is that what had you so upset?"

"It's my cousin Amber again. She's pregnant by Andre. Before he died, he left a will, and in it, he left her a large sum of money. I informed her not to tell Anton she was pregnant. She went to a meeting with them, and apparently, there was a special stipulation in Andre's will, giving her more money if she had a child. Well, she admitted to them that she was pregnant. Now Anton has hired all sorts of people for her. She has a full-time staff that waits on her hand and foot. She has a private doctor, and you ought to see her apartment. It's filled with all kinds of expensive baby things and she's only a month or so into her pregnancy. What she doesn't know is that this baby allows Anton into her life in ways she'll never understand. She should've kept the baby a secret and continued with her life. If she has a son, Anton will stop at nothing to get that baby away from her. He and his brother were the last two men in the Delgado family. Anton will take her baby. Trust me, and he doesn't have children of his own."

"Now I can understand your frustration. I would be upset too."

"Blaine, she keeps making these life-altering mistakes, and she won't heed my advice. She knows they're dangerous. She saw it first-hand, but she has gone over and sold herself and her child to the devil for a little money."

"Well, baby, as much as you hate it, she *is* an adult, and she can make her own choices. I don't want you to kill yourself worrying about her. You were so upset. Had that car been going any faster, you probably wouldn't be here. Now, I know Amber concerns you because she's your family, but my biggest concern is you. You're going to have to stop interfering with her life and allow her to make her own mistakes. I need you to stop doing that for me, for us, and for Amber. You see that no matter what you tell her, she is hell-bent on doing the opposite. Leave her alone for a while. She'll come around."

Cindy looked at Blaine. "Why did I know you were going to say that?"

"Because you know I'm telling you the truth."

Blaine put his arms around her. She laid her head on his shoulder. She knew he was right, but she was not about to let it go.

CHAPTER EIGHT

Cindy was home resting. Amber went by to check on her. Cindy was still upset with her. She didn't feel like communicating with her, but she allowed her to come inside. Cindy was lounging on the sofa. She wouldn't say much to Amber. Amber took a seat on the loveseat. She saw the bump on Cindy's head.

"Cousin, I know you don't approve of my decisions but…" Cindy interrupted her,

"Not now, Amber. I have a headache. I don't want to hear about your reasons or excuses."

Amber wrung her hands, trying to find the words to say to Cindy.

"I'm sorry about your accident. I can't help but feel it's my fault."

"Don't worry about it. I should've been watching where I was going. It was my fault."

Cindy quickly changed the subject and said to Amber, "You know what? I want to discuss your decision now that I think about it."

"Cindy, I'm doing what I feel is right for my child."

"No Amber, you're being greedy, selfish, and lazy. You want things handed to you on a silver platter. You want to take the easy way out; not realizing your choices will make your life difficult in the end. From the moment you began dating Andre, I warned you about the family and how dangerous they were. You refused to listen to me and went full speed ahead into the relationship with him. When things got difficult, you came running to me. I tried to help you. You got caught up with him again, and you were held against your will. You could've lost your life. When you found out they were offering money for your child, you sold yourself to the highest bidder not knowing that this is the biggest mistake of your life thus far. You refuse to listen. How does it feel to take money from a known criminal? .... You know what, don't answer that. I guess I can't blame you. The money is free, but what you don't know is that you will lose your child, the money, and possibly even your life. That baby doesn't belong to you. It belongs to Anton now. You won't be able to eat as much as a simple hamburger without him knowing. That's why he's hired all those people to look after you. It's not for you. This is his investment. You think you're being pampered and that he cares about you. He can give less than two fucks about you. You're nothing more than an incubator to him. Sure, enjoy all the spoils now, but once he gets his hands on that baby, you will be assed out. And you better not try to fight him. Anton Delgado will not think twice about either having you killed or doing something drastic and extricating you from your child's life. Oh, but you won't listen to me. You'll have to live it for yourself. Now, I

200

don't want to hear any more excuses from you, and I don't want to discuss this situation again. I've gotta get over the fact that you're going to do exactly what the fuck you want, and there's nothing I can say or do about it. I'm tired of worrying myself sick over you. Do whatever the hell you want. I'm done with it."

Cindy turned her back to Amber and lay on her side. Amber knew Cindy was upset. She dared not make any excuses. She understood how her cousin felt about the issue.

"I'm sorry that I'm such a big disappointment for you Cousin. I'm only trying to live my life. My boyfriend is dead, and I know I may not have loved him as I should've. I'm having mixed feelings right now. Then, I heard after his death that he genuinely loved me. I felt a sense of guilt." Cindy threw her hand up to say she didn't want to hear anymore. Amber tried to say something else, but Cindy interrupted her, saying,

"Enough, Amber; enough. You're giving me a fucking headache."

Feeling a little dejected, Amber turned around and sobbed a little. Amber put her feet up on the loveseat and they both took naps until Blaine came in and woke them. Cindy saw Amber lying on the loveseat. Her heart went out to her. Cindy had to remind herself that she was young and not street-smart. She was always pampered, being the only child of older parents. She hadn't lived the harsh street life that Cindy had. She didn't want her to follow in her footsteps. She wanted more than anything for her to realize the significance of her actions.

Amber looked up to Cindy and she admired her. She valued her opinion but was a bit headstrong as with most of the women in their family. Cindy was wiser and she knew her cousin felt she was doing the right thing. Cindy's mind flashed back to when her grandmother tried to tell her the truth about the streets, but she refused to listen and had to learn the hard way. But this was different. She was able to escape the dangers of street life and Delgado. Once she left him, she thought that part of her life was over, but it had come back to haunt her. If Amber had to go through what she'd gone through, Cindy knew the streets would've eaten her alive. She decided to stop preaching to Amber and do what she knew had to be done.

Blaine walked over to kiss her on the forehead.

"Baby, how are you feeling?"

"I'm doing much better." She stood to her feet.

"Amber, do you want to stretch out in the other room?"

"Yes, cousin, that would be nice." Amber went into the spare bedroom and immediately went back to sleep.

Cindy's body was sore from the accident, so she soaked in the tub for a while. Afterwards, she got her computer and began working on getting her club back up and running. She was putting together ads to hire more entertainers, chefs, wait staff, and bartenders for her club. After she was done, she got dressed and called Jessica.

"Jessica, this is Cindy. Blaine told me that you didn't just happen by the scene of the accident. He told me that you had been following me to protect me. I want to thank you for that, but I want to ask you not to follow me anymore. I feel that my privacy is being violated especially when I'm in the dark about what's going on."

Jessica said, "I understand how you could feel that way. I'm sorry we were only trying to help."

"Well, as much as I appreciate it, please, I'm begging you not to follow me anymore."

"I'll stop it. But be careful okay," Jessica warned.

"I've survived this long. I'll be alright, and if I need you, I hope I can still count on you."

"Why, of course, my friend, you know that."

Cindy laughed, "Thank you, girl. I'll chat with you later I have to go."

Now that Cindy had gotten Jessica off her trail, she called Detective Armstrong. "Hello, Armstrong"

"Is this Cindy?"

"You know it Sugar,"

"How are ya, Cindy?"

"It's been a rough year. I've been going through some things as you know. If it weren't for Blaine and Jessica looking out for me, I don't know where I'd be."

"Again, Cindy, I'm sorry for your loss."

"Thank you. That's what I'm calling about. How's the investigation coming along?"

"I wish I could give you some news, but we haven't made any progress on those cases. We still don't have any new leads."

"So, in so many words, someone has gotten away with killing two innocent people?"

"I wouldn't say that, Cindy. Eventually, they'll be caught. But in the meantime, we're doing everything we possibly can to bring their killers to justice."

"I understand," Cindy said. Cindy, knowing that she killed Andre, wanted to see if the police had any evidence leading to her, so she toyed with him mentioning the death. "What's going on with

204

Delgado's brother? I heard his brother was killed. What can you tell me about that?"

"Those cases are out of my jurisdiction. The FBI is handling both of those cases. We've found out through our sources that Anton Delgado is still alive. I think they may have found his new hiding spot. You know he's been on the run ever since that big dust-up over in Miami. I know you heard about it."

"Yes, I know more than you think I know," she said under her breath.

"What did you say?"

"Oh, nothing."

"Well, the Feds are hoping he'll come to them for help so they can draw out those hunting him. They want him to turn like his father did back in the day. That way, they could tie up loose ends to cold cases, and he would possibly give us information on his involvement."

"Well, I know Anton and I don't think he would ever turn to the Feds for help. He'd rather stay on the run. It's just not his style."

"Cindy, they seem to think it's worth a try."

"I can assure you; they'll be wasting their time. He's told me himself that he won't be caught dead in any prison system. He'd rather die first." Cindy changed the subject. I'm thinking about reopening my club. I want to know if it's safe to do so. I don't want any more shit. I've lost enough already, and a lot of people have been affected by these latest attacks on my business. Just trying to see if the department can beef up patrols and possibly hire some off-duty officers. I know you have some suggestions on who your favorites are for the job. Also, before I go, I want to ask you for a huge favor."

"What is it?"

"I want to know if you can look into the case of my son's death. The police and the fire department said it was an accidental fire. I want to know if you can check that out for me again, okay? Just once more to satisfy my curiosity."

"Okay, I'll see what I can do."

"Thank you, Sugar, I'll talk with you soon."

"Okay bye."

Cindy called Jessica again. She wanted Jessica to investigate the case of her son's death. She also spoke with Blaine about it in great detail. She got the old files from the basement of her home and gave them to Blaine to give to Jessica. As a favor to her, they immediately went to work on the case. While they were doing that,

206

she was preparing to make her final move. She called Big Dan and informed him that she may need him to watch her back. In the meantime, Amber had awakened from her nap. She went into the living room where Cindy was sitting.

"Cindy, I'm about to get ready to go to my place. Anton just called. He says he wants me to look at some property. He feels that I need a bigger place with more room. He's having a car come to pick me up."

This was the open-door Cindy needed. She understood that Amber was going to do what she wanted anyway, so she would use it to her advantage.

"Do you trust that he'll bring you back safely?"

"I have no reason to believe he wouldn't. He's too excited about this baby; he wouldn't do anything to jeopardize our safety. He acts as if he's the father. He's been so overprotective. He calls and checks on me all the time. He's not going to do anything."

Cindy didn't want to hear any of what Amber was saying, and she could tell by her foolish talk, that she hadn't listened to anything she'd been telling her.

"Well, let's be safe and put this in your purse so that if anything goes wrong, like the last time, someone will know where to find you."

"If you insist cousin. How many of those things do you have anyway? Do you just keep them lying around the house?"

"You know Blaine is a private detective. These things come to a dime a dozen. I just want you and the baby to be safe."

Cindy gave the tracking device to Amber's, and she headed home. Delgado sent a car for her as promised. She was taken to tour several properties. Delgado was in attendance, but he was in a separate vehicle. Afterward, he had her taken back to where he was staying. They ate dinner and he had the car take her home. Cindy had been monitoring the tracking information. She looked up the addresses. One address in particular where they'd stopped for a few hours was in a rural part of town called Mayflower. Cindy rode by the address and sure enough, she saw some of Delgado's men hanging out. She sat and watched for a while, and she left. Later she called Amber and asked her how everything went. Almost in a braggadocios tone, Amber told her of all the properties they went to visit. She was excited and still blinded by the money. Although she had her share of what Andre left, she couldn't get the baby's share until it was born, so having Delgado foot the bill for all her extravagant items where right up her alley.

She threw caution to the wind and was no longer afraid of him, especially since he was spoiling her. Through talking with Amber, Cindy gained valuable insight into who was in the home. She lay in wait. She watched the home continually for about a week. Everything was going according to plan.

She called Delgado and told him she wanted a meeting with him concerning the club. She wanted to lure him and his men away from the house, and she planned to ambush him on the street as she did when she assassinated his brother. He opted to talk to her by phone instead, so she called.

"Not long ago, you wanted to buy this place from me. You haven't spoken about it in a while. What do you want to do?"

"Cindy darling, I've had a lot to deal with. I haven't been able to talk much business lately. Things around me have been hectic. I'm in the process of trying to relocate. I plan on moving out of the state of Arkansas for a while. I'm going to lay low for a while until this war dies down."

"So, are you saying you're no longer interested in purchasing the club?"

"I'll have to get back to you on that," he said.

Cindy was livid because her friends died in vain. He wreaked havoc by negatively impacting many lives, and just like that, it was over. She was glad she could re-open the club without attacks, but she still wanted retribution for the lives lost.

"I'd like to thank you for looking out for my cousin. She's spoken well of you, and she told me how you've been taking care of her, especially during this time in her life. What are your plans once the baby is born?"

"This baby is a Delgado. After me, he's the only Delgado left. My plan is for him to carry on the Delgado legacy."

"So, you're saying you plan on taking a very active role in the child's life."

"Yes, I will. I feel I owe it to my brother and the Delgado family."

Cindy continued questioning him. None of his answers mattered because she knew he wouldn't be around to put them into action anyway. She just wanted confirmation of what she already knew. He would be taking over the life of the baby. She was tired of talking to him, so she ended the call. Her plan to ambush his car had been thwarted, but she didn't lose heart. She would try again, but she was beginning to grow weary of luring him to his death.

CHAPTER NINE

Jessica and Detective Armstrong were making progress on the case of Cindy's son and the nanny. They were able to come up with new leads. They went to the old neighborhood where the fire happened and spoke with the neighbors. Most were new residents of the area. Some who were there during the time of the fire refused to talk about the incident. They did, however, find one resident who was willing to speak with them. She was a seventy-year-old widow whose husband had died only months prior to their visit. Detective Armstrong introduced himself to her.

"Hi, ma'am; I'm Detective Byron Armstrong from the Little Rock Police Department's Major Crimes Division. This is Private Investigator Jessica Barnes. I want to know if we can have a minute of your time. We want to speak with you about a case that happened several years back." She looked at them both and breathed a sigh of relief. She motioned for them to come inside. Her Pomeranian dog barked at them as they entered the home.

"Hush up with all that racket," she said, yelling at the dog. She walked him into the other room and closed the door. "Y'all can have a seat. May I offer you something to drink?

"No ma'am, we're fine," Jessica said. The old lady sat on the sofa across from them and began speaking.

"I know why y'all are here. It's about that girl Leslie that got killed in that fire, her and that baby."

Detective Armstrong sat up in his seat. He and Jessica looked at each other. Detective Armstrong said, "Yes ma'am; how did you know?"

"I know because I saw the whole thing when it happened. I wondered when somebody would be smart enough to figure it out. That girl and that baby were murdered. That fire was intentionally set."

"What makes you say that, Ms. What's your name, ma'am?"

"My name is Ruthie Smith."

"Mrs. Smith, what makes you think they were murdered?"

"For about a week, this Hispanic guy had been hanging around. He was knocking on everyone's doors in the neighborhood, showing a picture of a mixed girl and her son. She moved in with Leslie. I met her once. I can't remember her name. But anyway, he showed me a picture of her, and I told him where she was staying. Later that night I was lying in my bed when I saw a large flash of light in my window. I got up to look and see what it was. Their house was on fire. I called the fire department and went out on my front porch. I heard a small explosion. That guy was standing there smoking a cigarette and smiling. He gave me a creepy look. As fire and rescue came, he had already left the scene. I was too afraid to tell them what I saw. I always feared I would be next. I kept quiet about it until now. That creepy look on his face was enough for me to stay quiet for the rest of my life. When I found out a little boy died in the fire, I felt horrible. I wanted to come forward back then, but I was afraid. I'm old now, and I'm about to die. I'm glad to tell you what I saw if it will bring justice. No, that fire was not an accident."

"Would you be able to point this man out if you saw him again?"

"Yes. I could never forget that face, those cold, evil eyes. You could look right through them and see his black soul. I had nightmares of him over the years, hoping never to wake and see him in my life."

"Ma'am, would you be willing to make a sworn statement about what you saw?"

"Yes, I will."

Detective Armstrong made provisions for her to be taken to the police department. She was shown pictures of the Delgado brothers but didn't identify them. They showed her photos of Wolf and others. She pointed Wolf out on the spot. "That's the guy right there," Mrs. Smith said. I'm willing to testify against him any day. As I said, I'm no longer afraid." Detective Armstrong looked at her and said, "Ma'am, you are quite brave, but your sworn statement is good enough for us. There won't be a trial because this guy is deceased." The old lady looked at the picture again.

"How did he die?"

"He was gunned down in his home. We're still investigating his death."

"Well, it serves him right. I'm ready to make my statement and leave if you're done with me. I have to feed my dog." They recorded her statement and had her taken back home. Jessica and Detective Armstrong were sitting in his office discussing the case.

"Can you believe Wolf killed Cindy's son?"

"I know; that's strange; isn't it? I wonder if Delgado ordered the hit?" Jessica, looking as if she was trying to figure things out, said,

"I wonder how Cindy knew about it. I mean, she came right to me and asked me to investigate the case. She told me they were killed. How did she find out?"

"When did she find out?"

"She wouldn't go into any details with me." He asked, "Why don't you chat with her and see if she'll tell you anything? She and I are cool, but you two have a special friendship. She's more likely to open up to you."

"I'll ask her when I see her," Jessica said. They had enough to reopen the case and reclassify the deaths as a homicide instead of accidental. They contacted the original investigators of the case to view what evidence was left. Wolf had discarded his cigarette butts at the scene, and they'd been saved. In the meantime, Amber was at Delgado's place. She'd been spending most of her time there and they were seemingly becoming close friends. Amber often stayed there many nights.

Jessica arrived at Cindy's place to brief her on what they found. Although she wasn't expecting any visitors, she invited her inside.

"Come on in girl. You have to excuse my mess." Cindy tried cleaning a little. Jessica was seated as she got some things out of the way.

"I stopped by to tell you what we found on the case of your son's death. You were right. The fire was no accident. We even found someone willing to testify. She was taken down to the precinct, and she identified Wolf in a photo line-up as the man who'd committed the crime. She said when she saw the fire, she called fire and rescue. When she came out to help, she said he was standing there smoking a cigarette. When the authorities came, he left. She said she was too afraid to come forth. She's speaking up and was willing to testify against him in court until we told her he was deceased. Cindy, how did you know the fire wasn't an accident?"

"I knew because my son's killer told me he did it. Yes, Wolf confessed to me while I was riding with him. He said he'd planned on killing me too. It just so happened I wasn't in the house. He says Anton didn't know anything about it, and he was acting of his own accord. He said I was getting in the way of Anton's business."

Cindy gripped her fist tight out of anger.

"Yeah, that smug bastard enjoyed telling me all about it. He gloated as he spoke, even threatening to kill me that night, but he let me go, and I…."

Cindy came to herself at that moment. Jessica, wanting her to finish her statement, asked, "What did you do, Cindy?"

"I went home and cried myself to sleep."

"So that's why you've been so upset lately."

"Yes, I've been coping with it. I couldn't go to the police because more people could've gotten hurt: my cousin, Blaine, or me."

Feeling sympathetic for her friend, she said, "I'm so sorry you've had to suffer this alone. You've been through so much lately. I know it seems as if the police couldn't do much, but without proof or a confession, their hands were tied."

Cindy asked,

"Would you like to know what else he confessed to?"

"Yeah, tell me."

"He confessed to killing my employees and acted as though their deaths were a waste of his time."

"Are you kidding? He told you he killed them?"

"Yes, but what can be done about it now? Even if I had gone to the police, there's still no proof, just my word against his, and he could claim I lied on him. So, there was nothing left to do but deal with it in my own way."

Cindy knew Jessica didn't know what she meant. She stopped short of telling her that she was responsible for the killings.

"I'm so sorry Cindy."

"Thank you, Jessica. There was nothing we could do. Even if I'd gotten a taped confession, they would still find a way to retaliate. People like that hold others hostage with seemingly no remorse.

217

They live their lives free and happy while wreaking havoc in the lives of others. Well, he won't get to terrorize anyone else. That's for sure."

"Cindy, even though he's dead, I think you should let Armstrong know that he confessed. Perhaps one day in the future, they'll be able to find more evidence and bring closure to the families as well as the case."

"Jessica, they've been killing for years. There will be no evidence. You do remember I lived with Anton, and I'm from the streets, I know how they operate. They will never be caught or jailed. They either die out or are killed by rivals. Wolf is dead and so is Andre. Their past caught up with them. They finally got what they deserved. Sometimes street justice is warranted."

"Looks like you're right," Jessica said.

"Cindy, do you think I could use your restroom? Girl, I've had several cups of coffee today."

"Sure, you can. The powder room's toilet is out of order. Randy is having a plumber come and take a look at it. You can use the one in the guest bedroom." Jessica made her way back to the guest bedroom. Jessica passed Cindy's room. She noticed a small arsenal lying on Cindy's bed. She also saw a red wig, some gloves, and other suspicious items that caught her attention. Cindy thought about the things she had lying on the bed, and she hurried to close her bedroom door. Jessica didn't mention what she saw to Cindy. She used the restroom and wondered to herself why Cindy needed so much firepower. She wondered what she could be hiding if anything. She wanted to probe a little deeper, but she waited and decided to watch her again. After she washed her hands, she walked back through the hallway. This time, she had planned on taking a closer look, but when she got to Cindy's room, she noticed the door was closed. Cindy, who was now back in the living room sitting, asked,

"Would you like some coffee? I'm having a cup."

"No, thank you. I've had my weight in coffee today. I wouldn't be able to get any sleep."

Cindy replied, "I haven't gotten any good sleep in months. I've almost forgotten what it feels like to sleep an entire night. I've been so stressed lately."

"Have you thought about taking something to help you sleep?" Jessica asked.

"Yes, but I still wake through the night. I tend to sleep better when Blaine is here. That is when he's not with his sons. Besides, as long as I'm dealing with this Delgado drama, it's not safe to have them over. Blaine insists on being here with me. He wants to protect me."

Cindy stood to her feet and said, "Perhaps we won't have to worry about that too much longer."

"What do you mean?" Jessica asked. Cindy brushed her off. "Jessica girl, I've let the time get away from me. I have a few things to take care of. I'll have to see you out for now, but get with me tomorrow, and we'll talk."

Cindy walked her to the door and let her out. Before Jessica left, she looked at Cindy and asked, "Cindy are you going to be okay?"

"Yes"

"Cindy, if you need me, give me a call."

"I will," she said; Jessica put her hand on her shoulder and said, "Cindy, I saw the weapons. What are you doing with so many guns? Do you feel you need all of that to protect yourself?"

Cindy looked her in the eyes and said, "I must do what's right. I need to do what's best for me."

"Cindy, don't do anything stupid; I don't want you to get hurt, okay." Cindy pursed her lips for a moment, and then she responded,

"Neither you, Blaine, nor the police department could protect my employees. If they want me, there's nothing neither of you can do to stop them. The only thing that would be left to do is clean up my corpse when they're done with me. Well, I don't intend on letting that happen."

"Cindy, I know you don't need my advice, and you're a tough woman, but you don't want to do anything you'll regret. Trouble is easy to get into and hard to get out of."

"Jessica, I have nothing to lose and everything to gain. My life was stolen from me when my son was taken, my friends are gone and I'm here like a sitting duck. No, sweetie, trouble came knocking at my door, and I plan on answering it my way. Now I said I have some business to attend to, and we'll chat tomorrow."

Jessica hesitated for a minute. Cindy's facial expression let her know she was serious. Jessica left. She knew Cindy was about to do something drastic and she didn't quite know what it was, but she had a sickening feeling in the pit of her stomach. She didn't want to lose her friend to violence or prison. She only hoped that Cindy would sit still and allow the police to handle things. She started her engine and drove away.

In the meantime, Cindy gathered her things and put them in her vehicle. She was about to make plans to get her a rental car, but before she could do so, Delgado called and asked to see her. She called her friend Big Dan and told him where she would be. She informed him that if anything were to happen to her, Delgado would be responsible. She gave him the address to his place.

She put on her thigh holster and her girdle outfitted with a holster and put her gun in it. She finally put on her bra which also had a hidden holster in it. She put a knife in a small purse. She drove over to the club, where he had a car to pick her up. She was driven to the home where he was staying. The driver let her out of the car. Armed men were everywhere. She took in a deep breath while surveying her surroundings. One of the armed men took her by the arm, led her to the front door, and let her in. Rita was standing at the door, and she escorted her into a den area of the home. When she looked up, she saw Amber sitting in a chair in lingerie. Amber appeared frightened but calm. Her eyes scanned the room as she followed Delgado's voice while he spoke.

"Hello, my darling Cindy," he said, looking as if he had caught her hand in the cookie jar.

"I'm so glad you came. I invited you here today because I want to discuss a few things with you."

She could tell his mood had shifted, and he was back in the driver's seat. The expression on his face was one he would give just before killing his opponent. Cindy looked up at the large television screen. There was a video playing with Delgado and Andre, celebrating Andre's birthday. They were toasting and telling jokes. She looked at the sinister expression on his face.

222

"Well, I'm here as you requested; what would you like to discuss with me?"

He reached down, touched Amber's shoulders, and massaged her. He rubbed her arms and playfully kissed her neck while looking up at Cindy.

"You know, in the bible, it was customary that when a brother dies or is killed, his brother should take his wife and marry her, go in unto her, and start a family to carry on that brother's name." He continued kissing Amber. He then reached further down and began fondling her breast.

He firmly squeezed one and said, "You know I did that last night. I took this sweet little pussy of my brother's, and I gave her all the Delgado dick she could handle. She moaned and squirmed as I fed her this pole. She really enjoyed herself. I see why my brother fell in love with her. Her little hot mouth is amazing. I'm going to enjoy fulfilling my biblical duty. Afterwards, you know what she told me?"

She said that you told her to put a tracking device on my brother's phone. Not long after that, my brother and my friend were killed. Who could've known that my brother would be on the road that fateful night? Only one person, and that's the one on the other end of that tracking device, which I suspect was you. Would you care to tell me what happened to my brother?"

"Anton, you've made many enemies. I'm just a lowly little owner of a bar. How could I come against an empire like yours, infiltrate it, and kill your brother? Are you serious? You give me too much credit." He walked over and picked up one of his swords and played with it.

"You know, I don't think I gave you enough credit." He took the sword and pointed it at Amber's belly. Now I'm going to ask you one more time. What happened to my brother?" She saw the terror on Amber's face.

"Your guess is as good as mine."

"I think you had my brother murdered." Cindy looked at him with a scowl on her face and said, "And I think you had my employees murdered. Wolf told me how he planned to betray you and take your empire. He told me that you had him kill my employees. He even confessed to killing my son and Ms. Leslie. He said he planned on killing me too, but I wasn't home that night. I've lost a lot over the years because of you. Now you bring me here, I guess to torment me. Why didn't you just kill me when you had the chance? You wait until I finally have a life and I'm doing well, and you turn my world upside down. Well, how does it feel to have someone attack your family or your friends? It's not so much fun, is it? You don't need to point your fingers at me; you should blame yourself and the life you chose to live. The majority of the people you've ordered killed were good, honest, hardworking people. They weren't in the game. They were making a living for their families. What did my employees ever do to you? They didn't deserve to die."

Delgado scoffed, "Oh, so you want sympathy from me? You know how I operate. I told you what would happen if you didn't do what I asked. Yes, I had them both killed. I warned the others that the same thing would happen to them. I couldn't kill all of them. That would've been too obvious. So, I put the fear of God in them. They got the message, took their payment, and moved on. Oh, and that Chef of yours, he was too good of a cook to kill. He works in one of my Miami restaurants. I made him such a lucrative offer that he couldn't turn it down. He sold you out so fast when he saw what I was offering, pretty much like your sweet little cousin over here. She sold your ass out. She almost fucked my brains out when she realized I could give her all the things she never had. She was so grateful to me, and she showed me just how much."

He grabbed the remote control and changed the video. He put on a video of him and Amber having sex. He narrated everything on the screen.

"Take a look. She really knows how to appreciate a man. Watch her work. He reached down and groped his penis.

"Oh, she can really take it all in. And there she is thanking me personally and begging me for more."

Cindy looked at him and said,

"Is that supposed to faze me in some way or another? I don't give a damn about you. Do you think this is supposed to bother me? Well, it doesn't. I would have to have feelings for you which I don't. You disgust me. I wonder how your brother would've felt about your betrayal. I do, however, feel sorry for Amber, who had to endure sleeping with a fucking mutt. Yeah, you may think you're the cream of the crop, but you have no class. You're just a mutt with cash, a bully who must pay women and young girls to sleep with you. I was young when we got together. I didn't know any better, but I do now, and every time I think of having slept with you, I cringe. Just because you can afford to buy and sell people, you should know that you can't buy loyalty. Wolf was going to team up with Cash, kill you and your brother, and take over your organization. Oh, and half of your workers were placed here by Wolf. Am I right?" Delgado looked around at his guys. He knew she was right.

"I wonder how many of them are truly loyal to you? Will they kill you, and take over as planned? Can you trust everyone in your camp? Perhaps they're watching your back to stab you in it. I can only imagine which one is thinking you're better off dead than alive. It's good for you that Wolf died when he did, or you'd probably already be dead."

"I have no need not to trust my men. They've been loyal to me, and they'll continue to do so."

She shrugged her shoulders and said, "If you say so." She looked at the screen as the video was still playing.

She looked at Amber and said, "Great job Amber. I see you have the family gene in you. You know how to fuck a man and change his world. We got power in our pussies. I'm so proud of you." She winked at Amber, and she asked Delgado,

"Now, is there anything else you would like to discuss because I have shit to do today?" Delgado was furious.

"Cindy, I didn't bring you here to talk. He walked over to her and tried to kiss her on the lips. She bit his bottom lip and clenched it between her teeth. She wouldn't let go. He grabbed her around the throat and tried to choke her. She peeled his fingers away and bit down harder on his lip. Rita came over and pulled her off him. He slapped her.

"You bitch! I ought to kill you right now."

"Why don't you, you fucking coward?" He looked at Rita. When we're done here, I want you to take her out back and kill her ass. I think it's time I rid myself of this problem once and for all. I tried being nice, but you want to play hardball. It's time we end this.

But first I want to tell you the plans I have for your sweet little cousin here. I'm going to take good care of her. I'm going to enjoy fucking her for the next few months until she drops this load. After that, I'm going to kill her too and bury you bitches in the same fucking hole; Now Rita take this trash out."

Rita walked over to Cindy and grabbed her by the arm and walked her toward the door. Cindy looked at him and said, "Why don't you kill me yourself?"

Cindy unexpectedly snatched away from Rita. She dropped to the floor pulling Rita down with her. She immediately grabbed her gun out of her thigh holster and began firing at Delgado. She hit him in the shoulder and the leg. He immediately fell to the floor. Amber sprinted from her seat and ran towards Cindy. Delgado's men came running in to see what was happening. Cindy grabbed her other gun and began firing on them as they made their way into the room killing anyone who entered. She yelled at Amber,

"Get their guns!" Amber was frantic. She took the guns off the men as they fell inside the door. Rita began to make her way to her feet.

"Bitch don't make me kill you," Cindy said to Rita. Cindy hit her in the head with the butt of her gun and tripped her and she fell back to the floor. Cindy grabbed Amber by the arm and hid behind the door.

"If anyone comes in here, you start firing at will. She took her cell phone out and called Big Dan. He was on standby, and he began firing on everyone who was stationed outside so that Cindy could make her way of escape. Delgado looked at Rita and screamed,

"Get up bitch!" He tried to scoot over to her to check her for a weapon. He was bleeding profusely from his wounds. He had the use of only one arm and one of his legs. He smeared blood all over the floor as he dragged his body across the room. He pulled himself up on the sofa and tried to reach the cabinet where he kept a pistol. Cindy noticed him reaching for the cabinet and shot him in the hand. She kicked him around looking at the door and watching Amber to make sure she was okay. As Delgado's men barged into the room, a frightened Amber managed to shoot everyone who came in the door, killing four of them. She grabbed their weapons and emptied them on the next round of guys coming in. They heard a barrage of gunfire and several small explosions. The gunfire was getting closer, which frightened Amber all the more, but she was ready. Cindy had two guns, one pointing down towards Rita and the other on Delgado. "I've come here to kill you. Of course, I hadn't planned on coming here. I thought I would have to lure you out, but you invited me right in. I thank you for that."

"Bitch, you're a nobody. You're a fucking washed-up whore. You ought to feel honored that I gave you a second look. I should've pimped your ass out, but I wouldn't get anything for you because your pussy is trash. I bet your grandmother's pussy feels better, perhaps she's taken a few less dicks than you." Cindy shot him in the stomach. He howled in pain. She leaned over and whispered to him so nobody else could hear her,

"I killed your bitch-assed brother. I shot and killed Wolf. I killed Cash, and I blew your fucking home up in Scott. I killed all your men. Not bad for a fucking washed-up whore, huh? And to make my day even better, I'm going to kill you too. She stood up from her stooping position and placed the heel of her foot in his wound. She stepped on top of him and walked over to the other side. He looked up at her and said, in Spanish, *"No te saldras con la tuya!"* As to say, "You won't get away with this."

She smiled and said, "I believe I already have." She shot him in the groin. With each bullet she fired, she gained pleasure watching him fight for his life. She could see the fear in his eyes. She knew at this moment that this was what she was meant to do. This would be the end of her problems. She replayed all the evil times she had spent with this ruthless killer. She knew if she didn't kill him, he would kill her and her family. If she allowed him to live, she'd never be able to live a life of quality. She refused to spend the rest of her life looking over her shoulder. She reached into her bra and took out her gun and aimed it over his head. Just as she was about to fire, she heard Jessica's voice calling her name.

"Cindy, don't, honey. Don't kill him. You'll hate yourself in the morning. We have the place secure, and the police are on the way."

"Jessica if you're truly my friend, please, you won't deprive me of this. I've been through too much. He's caused me too much pain and misery. I must kill him. If I don't, I'll never be rid of him." Delgado was still screaming in pain from his wounds.

"You better kill me now bitch, because if you don't, I'm definitely going to kill you. If it's the last fucking thing I do." She kicked him in the jaw.

"Shut the fuck up you bastard." He reached for her leg and tried with all his strength to pull her to the floor. She struggled to get her leg loose. Cindy looked down at him, pulled the trigger, and shot him in the face. Amber made a high-pitched scream. Delgado stopped moving.

Cindy went over to Amber and held her close to her bosom.

"Are you okay, sweetie?" Still trembling, Amber nodded her head and began crying. Jessica went over to check Delgado's pulse. He was dead. Rita began to regain consciousness. She looked around and saw the chaos in the room. She noticed Delgado's body and then her eyes went to Cindy and Amber. Jessica was standing over Rita with the gun still in hand. She leaned over to reach for her helping her to her feet. Jessica allowed Rita to lean on her for support.

Amber noticed Jessica helping Rita and yelled, "Why are you helping that bitch? She's one of them. She's the enemy. She works for Anton. Jessica said, "Calm down. She's okay." Jessica began checking Rita for injuries. She said, "Agent Stokes, that's a nasty knot on your forehead."

"It hurts like hell too," she said to Jessica.

"I didn't know you were working this case." Jessica helped her over to a stable seat until they could get her help. Agent Amy Stokes looked at Cindy and said, "Girl you have a helluva right. You hit me so hard that you knocked me unconscious. Shit, I'm glad you didn't shoot me." Cindy apologized. She, too, was relieved she hadn't shot the agent.

"I'm agent Stokes, known to you, Amber, as Rita. I've been on this case for a while now."

Amber looked at her, and said, "I knew you weren't just a maid. You didn't look the part."

"I was assigned to work this case from the inside."

Jessica was glad to see everyone was okay. Blaine ran into the room. He was dirty and bore scratches from debris during the mayhem. He stepped over the bodies of Delgado's men and immediately went to Cindy.

"Baby, I'm so glad you're okay. What in the hell were you thinking, coming here alone? Why didn't you let us know what was happening? And before you ask how we knew you were here, yes, we followed you. Jessica and I were concerned for your safety." She held him close and said, "It's over baby. It's finally over."

She looked back at Anton Delgado's body. Blaine walked her out of the room. Everyone made it outside. The police and ambulance were on the scene as well as the fire department. Big Dan was outdoors. Paramedics were treating him for minor wounds. He wore a black T-shirt. There were a few holes in it from the gunfight and scuffle with several of Delgado's men. Cindy went to him and hugged him.

"Big Dan, are you okay?"

"You know I'm okay. A few of them tried to tackle me at once, but I got them straightened out real quick. Girl, you know Big Dan doesn't fall that easy. It's gonna take more than a few chumps like them to stop me. There they are over there lying beside those vehicles. There's no telling where the rest of them are. Your friends showed up and helped, and afterward, the police came." Cindy held him tightly.

"I'm so glad you're okay," she said. The police took everyone's statements. Agent Amy Stokes told her version of events and explained that Cindy was brought there against her will that their lives were in danger, and that she killed the men in self-defense. With all the weapons floating around and knowing Delgado dealt with illegal weapons, Cindy wasn't questioned about the guns. They all went to the police department to make their official statements. Cindy was cleared to go home, and the case was closed after a few months. Delgado admitted to killing Cindy's employees in the presence of the FBI agent. Although he would never serve a day in jail for the crimes, Cindy knew justice had been served.

Over the next few weeks, she began to plan for the grand re-opening of the club and restaurant. Amber had her share of Andre's money and was expected to get the baby's share. She sold both condos and went back to law school. Cindy called her down to do a show with her. Amber was excited to be a part of it. She was given her script and Cindy had a wardrobe made for her. Amber's pregnancy was not yet showing, and she had a very thin frame so it would be no problem for her to perform. Life was back to normal, and Cindy couldn't be happier. She and Blaine were closer than ever and more in love. They discussed the possibility of starting a family. Cindy was open to the suggestion.

In the meantime, Jessica was out with Marcus and her parents for dinner. Her parents were constantly flirting and kissing.

Jessica looked up from the dinner table and said, "You guys, Get a room already."

Her mother said, "Girl, hush. Leave us grown folks alone. Can't you see we're in love?" She kissed Jack again. Jack got up from his seat and began to talk to her mother.

"Baby I want to ask you if you would marry me again. This time, I'll be a better husband to you. I'll be the man you deserve. I want to live the rest of my life with you. I let you get away once; I don't plan on that ever happening again." He slipped the ring on her finger.

"Annie, say you'll spend the rest of your life with me." She smiled and looked at her ring.

"Of course, I will. I love you." They kissed and Jessica and Marcus congratulated them.

She hugged both her parents and said, "Now, you two play nice this time." They all laughed.

Jessica was seated and Marcus stood to his feet. Jessica looked at him and asked, "Marcus where are you going?"

He took her hand and said, "Jessica Barnes, it's no secret the love I have for you. From the moment I met you, I knew I had to make you mine even if I had to spend the rest of my life in pursuit of you. You gave me the opportunity to show you that I was worthy of your love. Will you give me the same opportunity of becoming your husband? I'll be good to you, and I'll definitely be good for you. If you say yes, I promise I'll never let you regret it." She smiled at him and said,

"You think so, huh? You're that sure of yourself?"

He looked into her eyes and said, with a sincere heart, "I love you enough to do all I need to keep you in my life and ensure your happiness. I love you, Jessica."

She smiled and batted her eyes, "Well since you put it that way, I'll have to say yes." He slipped a custom-designed, three-carat, emerald-cut, diamond ring on her finger. She looked at it and said,

"Damn baby, you're off to a great start!! I love it. I think I'm going to enjoy being married to you. They kissed passionately. Her mother cleared her throat.

"Do you two need a room dear?"

"Oh, Mom, give us a break; can't you see we're in love?"

They enjoyed their evening. Unbeknownst to Jessica, Marcus went to her father asking for his blessing to marry her. He gladly obliged. The two men had carefully planned the idea of proposing to their loves. A celebration was in order, and they did just that.

~THE GRAND REOPENING~

Cindy spared no expense on the new shows. She called in several Hollywood celebrities from the "A" list actors to chart-topping hit recording artists. She had plaques made up as a memorial for her son Micah, her employees Michael and Angelica, as well as Ms. Leslie. She invited their loved ones, and she opened the club with a moment of silence for each one. A tribute was done and afterward, a song was performed. Once that was over, the real show began. The celebrities were invited to do several skits and dances in what was to be one of the best, show-stopping, grand stage performances. Cindy came out at the end and performed her signature piece for her love of Blaine.

Afterward, she and Amber put on a show dressed in tight, sexy bodysuits—Cindy's was black, and Amber's was white. The poem was titled "Love Battle." It's about two women fighting for the love of a man. They recited the poetry while acting it out on stage. The sexy shirtless male performer would dance with Cindy and recite poetic promises to her, and then when Cindy turned her back to him, he slowly danced over to Amber.

The lights were on him as he danced erotically with Amber and recited the same poetic promises to her that he had to Cindy's character. The women pretended to battle each other for his love. After realizing he was playing them both, they pretended to kill him.

In the end, both women were free. The performance was a hit with the women in the audience.

There were also comedy skits and stand-up comedians. The show was amazing, and everyone spoke about it for weeks. Since Cindy hired a videographer to record the show, it was placed online for sale. The celebrities involved blogged about it and sent word letting Cindy know they were available to work with her anytime she needed them. After the word spread of the club, Cindy's fame spread, and her club was on the list of the must-see shows in the state. Also, several people requested that she take her shows on the road. She kept her options open, but for now, she opted to stay in her state of Arkansas, which was a much sweeter place to be, now that the Delgados were gone.

ABOUT THE AUTHOR

Karen Coleman is an Arkansas native. She enjoys writing exciting and dramatic stories. A phenomenal author with a distinctive style, she has demonstrated a sensational talent for steering her readers through every line and page with eager anticipation.

Karen has published several novels in various genres. Readers have described her novels as riveting, fast-paced, and thrilling reads.

Her teen novels are insightful and empowering. As a mentor who has worked with teens for many years, Karen understands the social challenges they face, and she skillfully addresses those topics with a finesse that lends excitement, adventure, and encouragement.

A self-proclaimed fiction writer with an element of truth, Karen began penning her thoughts as a hobby. After many years of writing and encouragement from those around her, she began writing more intensely, eventually turning out several wonderful novels. She offers something for almost every reader; from her adult crime series to her teen books, there's something to be enjoyed by all. Her literary works have garnered much fanfare and have only been enjoyed by her many readers; she's highly celebrated among her writing peers. Her books are meant to inspire, uplift, and entertain, leaving her audience asking for more.

Karen is also a playwright, actor, and former city council member. She's the mother of four and a Glam-ma of thirteen and counting. Her grandchildren affectionately call her Nana. She's also the proud mom of two rambunctious miniature schnauzers. She spends time crafting, fishing, or enjoying a great barbecue when not writing or spoiling her grandbabies.

Other Books by the Author

Closer Than Enemies 1&2

Metamorphosis "Good Girl Gone Bad"

Whatever Happened to I love you?

No Place for Emily Ann

Arkansas Heat "A City Scorned"

Arkansas Heat "A Brutha's Obsession"

Arkansas Heat "Cindy's Revenge"

Arkansas Heat "Raising Delgado

Arkansas Heat "Deceptive Practice"

In The Wrong Game

Morgan's Path

Frozen Dreams

I Am a Whole Being "Finding Wholeness after Rejection, Abandonment, Pain, and Loss"